THE LAST LIE

A Baker Girls Romance

BETHANY MONACO SMITH

ABOUT THE LAST LIE

The Last Lie is the first book in the Baker Girls interconnected standalone series. All books in the series can be read as standalone novels.

The Last Lie is a low angst, vacation rom-com featuring professional quarterback Mark, and workaholic social worker Frannie, who meet on a plane on the way to the same little beach town. *The Last Lie* is full of sexual tension, beach vibes, hilarious banter, and plenty of steamy and swoony moments.

Ready to fall in love with Mark and Frannie?

MEET THE CHARACTERS

The love interests in desperate need of a vacation:
Mark Abbott
Frannie Baker

The Baker Girls:
Kennedy Baker
Hallie Baker

Mark's family/friends:
Ryan Hardison (Hardy)
Brian Ackley
Rae (McKinley) Cooper
Dani Malone
Sarah McKinley
Pete & Bea Abbott (The Best Grandparents Ever)

TRIGGER WARNINGS

If you're looking for possible triggers in this book, this page is for you. If you're not, you can skip this page and dive into the story.

trigger warnings may contain plot spoilers

As a lighthearted read, I tried my best to keep this one as trigger-free as possible. The following things are only briefly mentioned/discussed: witness to/stopping of sexual assault (not involving a main character), domestic abuse (mentioned)

Any updates or changes to this information can be found at bethanymonacosmith.com/triggers

To anyone (like me) who is terrified to fly on a plane.
Let this be your encouragement to give it a try. ;)

CHAPTER ONE
SUNDAY

"MARK ABBOTT HAS DUG *himself a deep hole. The second-string quarterback for the New York Bandits is under scrutiny after getting into a fistfight with starting QB and team captain, Jeff Rucker, over wanting more playtime during the Super Bowl. The team ended up in a brawl that led to division on the field and cost them the game. The blame rests solely on this young quarterback's shoulders. Despite it only being his second season in the league, this could be viewed by some as a career ender.*"

Ignoring the TV playing this crap, I pull my baseball cap down farther, thankful my curly hair is mostly hidden and my black eye is barely noticeable anymore.

The airport is the worst place to be as tabloid fodder, but a little while longer and I'll be on the plane to one of the few safe spaces I have left.

My coach warned me this would happen, especially given the fight.

"Don't worry about it, son. The vultures will move on to someone else in a few days. When the story breaks in a few weeks and the truth comes out, you'll be the hero, not the villain. Just lie low until then."

That was a week ago, the day after we lost the Super Bowl. Unlike the rest of the world, my coach doesn't blame me. Half of my teammates do, but they're the ones who don't know the truth. That their revered, beloved QB is a monster who beats his wife and has sexually assaulted at least one young woman. I'm betting on more.

Contrary to what the reporters think, I don't mind riding the bench, but there's only so much I can goddamn take him walking by me and spewing on the sidelines. If that fucker hadn't mentioned the girl's name, the girl I ripped his drunken, half-naked body off of, maybe I could've gotten through watching him play one last time. But he said it, and I made him fucking regret it.

Of course, he has no idea how much he's going to regret what he did when he finds out the truth. I wasn't alone when I caught him the night before the Super Bowl. He was drunk and ended up in the wrong room. One that belonged to a newer kid on the team, Ryan Hardison, who we all call Hardy. Hardy, Brian Ackley —a first year newbie—and I were heading back to Hardy's room to decompress and chill with some beers and action movies when we found the "leader" of our team holding a woman down against her will on the bed. She was hitting him, screaming at him to stop as he shoved his hand between her legs.

After I pulled him off and threatened to beat his ass, he laughed it off. Brian—a two-hundred-forty-pound lineman—got Jeff the fuck out of there, while Hardy and I talked with the woman. Then we got Brian, and the four of us went right to our coach's room and told him what happened.

Jeff is one of many who subscribes to the bullshit professional sports "camaraderie" of don't ask, don't tell. As long as someone is a great player, everyone looks the other way if they cheat on their wife or dabble in sexual assault here and there.

I do not subscribe to that.

Not anymore. I made the mistake of following that party line in college when one of the guys on the team was accused of raping a girl at a party. It felt a little wrong in my gut, but I ignored the feeling and went on spouting off about how the girl was probably lying and trying to destroy his career before he ever had one.

I wasn't raised to pull that shit, but I'd been indoctrinated into the boys' club, and I was looking at hitting the draft the following year—which I did. I didn't want to make waves. But then I went to my grandparents' for a family gathering. My grandfather asked me about it, and I said the same thing I'd been saying... the girl was probably a liar and she was going to destroy my teammate's life.

The room fell silent and everyone's eyes were on me in disbelief. My grandfather—who is never to be trifled with—opened his mouth to speak, but before he could, my cousin lit into me. Screaming about what a piece of trash my teammate was and how disgusting it was that I was worried about his future being destroyed when he'd destroyed the girl's life. She stormed out.

Then my grandfather took me for a walk. Pete Abbott is many things, but above all else, he's a patriarch, and he does not hesitate to let anyone in his family know when they're fucking up. He said a lot of things, but one stuck with me over everything else.

"Who you are matters, Mark. You want to play a game you love? Do that. But you need to decide whether you're willing to sacrifice who you are, your morals, and your heart in the name of it. Don't become an asshole trying to fit in. You might think you'll find your place with them if you do, but you'll lose it with the people who really matter."

Then he walked away from me and left me to think. Thinking is about all I did for a couple of months. I avoided anything with the team that wasn't essential. Finally, I grew some balls and went to see my cousin, only to learn that she had been sexually assaulted. That was the last piece of the puzzle for me.

It's easy to avoid the truth when it's a faceless person—someone who doesn't exist in your reality. It sucks that it took hearing that for me to stand up, but I finally did. And I set a precedent on the team when I told my teammate to stop talking shit about the girl and that he should be ashamed of himself.

I made the right call because he was eventually arrested for raping her and was kicked off the team. From then on, I vowed to do the right thing. And I have.

Our coach wasn't surprised by what we told him, but more by the fact that we were telling him at all. He'd had suspicions about Jeff for a while. He'd see women crying as they left his room, but Coach had no evidence. No one on the team dared to go against Rucker.

When the girl—who was a staff member at the hotel we were staying at—said she wanted to file a report, it spurred Coach Robbins into following up on his greatest concern about Jeff. For some time, he'd believed Rucker was abusing his wife, but she always flashed a smile and played it off.

Coach had a long phone call with her and told her what had happened—that the girl would be filing a report. After Coach offered to help keep Jeff's wife safe, she broke down and admitted the truth. Jeff had been abusing her for years.

It was the night before the Super Bowl, but Coach Robbins stayed up half the night talking with both women, making sure they had safe places to go and the resources they needed, so when the woman he assaulted files a police report and his wife files for divorce, they'll be safe and Jeff will be blindsided.

Because Coach didn't want to tip Jeff off—he didn't want to give him a chance to pay people off—he let him play in the game, pretending everything was normal. Afterward, he quietly asked the athletic commission to look into Jeff's past behavior.

Maybe Coach should want to protect the team, but proving

he's a better man than most, he made it clear he wants Jeff to get the punishment he deserves.

Going along with all that, I'm taking the heat for the fight and any other problems with the team until the private investigator hired to look into Jeff releases his report and this all goes public within the next week or two.

At least the season is over and I can get the hell out of New York.

Not soon enough.

A guy walks past me and does a double-take.

Shit.

He shakes his head at me, grimacing.

"You'll be the hero, not the villain."

Right now, I'm public enemy number one.

I have no regrets. I know I made the right decision, but helping the number one team in New York State lose the Super Bowl and being considered the biggest asshole in the NFL is not pleasant.

"Flight 362 to Charleston International Airport now boarding," a voice says through the PA system.

Finally. I need a fucking vacation.

CHAPTER TWO

Frannie

YOU WILL BE FINE, *Frannie. You will not die in a fiery plane crash.*

I glance out the plane window and glimpse the tarmac. My stomach twists. If a chill goes up my spine seeing the ground directly under the plane when I look out the window, what's going to happen when I look out and see only sky?

Another chill. More nausea. Palms sweating.

What the hell was I thinking taking my first plane ride ever *by myself?* What was I thinking traveling so far for my first ever solo vacation—my first vacation at all in five years. There's something wrong with me.

Digging my phone out of my bag, I connect to the inflight Wi-Fi and open up messenger and find the group chat with my little sister, Hallie, and our cousin, Kennedy. Hallie is three years younger than me at twenty-three. Kennedy is two years older at twenty-eight. Despite me no longer living in the same city as them, we're still close as ever.

> This was a mistake. I'm on a plane. A PLANE!

HALLIE

Good morning to you, too, big sis.

> Hallie!

HALLIE

What do you want me to do? I'm not there.

> Say something calming.

KENNEDY

Why would you ever expect her to say something calming? She's chaos incarnate.

HALLIE

Hey!

KENNEDY

Don't act like it's not the truth.

> Can we get back to me? First, I messaged both of you because I'm freaking out. Second, Hallie, you work with kids! You're a nanny, for God's sake. You must be calming with them.

HALLIE

Kids are easy. Sing them a song. Talk about Bluey. Done. I'm the mouthy chaotic one. You two are the calm ones.

KENNEDY

See. I told you. I'm by far the more comforting one. Plus, I've ridden on way more planes than either of you. Yeah, they're flying metal death boxes, but only if you crash.

> You're right. This was a mistake. Enjoy your days. See you at my funeral.

HALLIE

If you're dead, technically you won't.

I'll be haunting you.

KENNEDY

At least we'll still get to see you.

HALLIE

Take a chill pill. Or get a drink. Relax. Have
fun. Oh, kids are done with breakfast. Gotta
go. Love you!

Grumbling, I close the app and turn off my screen, tossing my phone back into my bag.

It used to be when I felt like this, the first person I'd call was my mother. She always soothed me, but that was back before I learned she'd been lying to me my whole life.

I grew up thinking my mom was my mom and my dad was my dad. Then one day I was looking through old photos and figured out my dad wasn't my biological father. I confronted them, and my mother reluctantly confirmed it. When I asked why she never told me, I assumed my biological father was dead or in prison or was a one-night stand who never knew about my existence.

The actual reason? My mom didn't like him. Said he wasn't supportive during their relationship, so she broke up with him, then moved out without telling him where she was going.

To say I was angry and devastated would be a massive under-statement. Our relationship hasn't been the same since. She gave a halfhearted apology, but she felt like she'd done the right thing, no matter how unfair it was to me.

The only good thing that came out of it was that I was able to get in contact with my biological father. Though he admitted to being a shitty boyfriend at the time, he got his life together. He's married now with two other kids and is a college professor. He's kind and a good listener. I love my dad—the man who raised me —but spending time with my biological father has also shown me what I missed out on. There's so much of him in me, and it breaks my heart we were robbed of that relationship. Especially since he'd searched for me throughout my life, but since he couldn't afford a PI to hunt my mother down, he didn't have any luck.

If he weren't in class, I'd send him a message.

Still, I almost reach for my phone. I'm sure my mother would still have something calming to say. But I don't do it. That's the power of a lie—it can destroy everything. Which is why I try never to do it. I'm not one of those ruthless people who say whatever they're thinking, even if it's mean, but I try to be honest and genuine with everything I do.

Shaking my head, I take a deep breath. I still need a distraction, so I let my mind wander. Of course, the first place it goes is to my job.

I stop myself from checking my phone for any important work emails. My boss nearly had to throw me out of the office for this vacation, but I can't help it. I love what I do. It can be bleak at times, working for child protective services, but I make it my mission to help the kids I serve as much as humanly possible.

It's my third year on the job after moving away from Manhattan to the small town of Ida in upstate New York. I'd be lying if I said what happened with my mother wasn't part of the reason I moved. I'm also an introvert with a capital I, so the massive city I grew up in never felt like home. I enjoy the small-town vibes and cozying up with a good book by my living room window that overlooks the river.

That is what I should be doing right now. Having a nice staycation. Instead, I'm trapped in a flying death box all because a friend recommended a tiny, off-the-beaten-trail beach town an hour and a half south of Charleston.

You will not die in a fiery crash, I repeat again, letting my eyes slip closed as I take a few deep breaths.

Do I know that, though? For sure?

My breaths are sharp and forced and my legs are bouncing. Palms are sweaty.

Great. Now I have *Lose Yourself* stuck in my head.

There are footsteps up the aisle, then rummaging in the compartment above me.

I'm still internally singing along to Eminem. Weirdly, it's helping.

More movement—someone sitting down next to me.

And I'm sitting here like a psycho, rocking back and forth to an Eminem song playing in my head while trying to quell a panic attack of epic proportions.

A throat clears.

"Are you okay?" The voice I hear is deep and rumbling with a touch of a whisper, like he's trying not to draw attention to the fact that I look like I belong in a psych ward.

Finally—reluctantly—I flash my eyes open.

I stop moving. Eminem stops rapping in my head. Everything is silent and calm as I take in the heart-stoppingly-gorgeous man sitting next to me.

He's tall. Even sitting down, I can tell that much. I have to look up to see his face, and his long legs are stretched out in front of him. He's wearing a ball cap pulled down low, but I can still make out his features. Square jawline with the tiniest amount of reddish-brown stubble. Hazel eyes. Some auburn curls sticking out beneath his hat. A perfect nose. Raised eyebrows.

Shit.

He just asked if I'm okay, and now I'm shamelessly eye-fucking him.

No, I am not okay. I clearly need a psych eval.

My eyes meet his and some red creeps up his cheeks. He looks uncomfortable. Probably because I'm being a massive weirdo.

"I um—" I stammer. *Smooth.* "I'm okay. Just nervous. I've never flown before."

"Oh." He does a little laugh-sigh thing that shouldn't be sexy but absolutely is. Relief washes over his face. "I get that. It used to freak me out, too, but I had three older siblings to pick on me about being scared, so I got over it quickly. I don't necessarily recommend that method, but it did help."

For the first time, I relax a little and manage a small laugh. "My sister and cousin already heckled me via text. I'm glad they're not here."

He finally lifts his hat, and I get a good look at his features. A smile that is as stunning as the rest of him lights his entire face. "Well, I'm happy to indoctrinate you to the world of flying. I promise not to tease you if you get scared. And if the window seat bothers you, we can switch."

My cheeks heat, and I feel a smidge ridiculous. "Thanks..."

"Oh. Mark." He extends his hand. "Mark Hainley."

I awkwardly wipe my sweaty palm on my pants, then shake his hand.

"Frannie Baker."

"Nice to meet you, Frannie. I promise this won't be too bad once you get used to it."

"I hope you're right about that."

He flips his hand over on the armrest, his palm turned up.

"If you get scared, just take my hand."

My eyes drift down to his hand, taking in the deep lines on his palm and the rough skin of his fingers.

I look back up at him. "Okay. Thanks."

Since the plane has finished boarding, we both fasten our seatbelts. I look around at the business class section of the plane. It's not one of the fancy new ones that has all kinds of bells and whistles, but it has what I'm assuming are faux leather seats, extra leg room, and a large arm rest nestled between Mark and me—where his hand is still resting.

Well, at least if I die in a fiery plane crash, I'll die holding hands with a god-like man.

I take a deep breath, but before I can let it out, the plane moves—backward.

Grabbing the upturned hand next to me, I shut my eyes

tightly. But what shocks me more than the plane moving backward is the crackling electric energy of his palm pressed against mine. I feel like I put my hand on one of those paddles that you use to shock people's hearts. This is definitely a shock. A shock to my senses and a shock to my heart.

Deep laughter comes from the seat next to me, temporarily distracting me from the skin searing against mine.

"Why are we moving backward?" I whimper.

"The plane has to move away from the terminal to get to the runway. They typically go backward to do that."

I squeak out some nonsense noise, then the plane stops again.

I let out a deep breath, then slowly open my eyes and look over at Mark. His eyebrows are up and he is losing the battle of not laughing at me.

My fingers are still clawing into his hand—so hard that the tips of his fingers are turning white.

I'm insane.

I loosen my grasp, but don't let go, because now the plane is moving forward.

"No one told you how this works, huh?"

I shake my head. I was too chicken to even do research about it because I was afraid I'd talk myself out of it.

"Okay, maybe if I prepare you, you'll be a little less terrified with each thing that happens."

"Okay..." I breathe.

"First, we'll move slowly as we get to the runway we'll take off from."

As he finishes saying the words, the plane changes direction, inching forward, and my stomach tightens. I shouldn't have done this. Not even for a second.

"Breathe, Frannie." His dulcet voice is soft and calming, taking the edge off my frayed nerves.

I glance over at him, and he continues explaining.

"When the runway is clear, we'll pick up speed and you'll feel the plane lift off. There might be some bumpiness when that happens, but then we'll even out and unless we hit any turbulence, it should be a smooth flight."

"What about the landing?"

He gives me an impish smile. "Let's cross that bridge when we come to it."

I whimper again.

"If it helps, I've been on a lot of flights, and the worst I've ever experienced is some rough turbulence."

I nod, but can't seem to let go of his hand.

"Thank you. You didn't have to be nice to the crazy stranger sitting next to you."

He laughs. "I was a kid when I flew the first time, but it still scared me. It would've sucked to have to go through that alone."

"Still... I don't know. You seem like a nice guy."

He chuckles. "You sound surprised. Run into a lot of assholes?"

"No. Just wasn't expecting to end up sitting next to a guy who offered to hold my hand—oh crap!"

The plane lurches forward. It's moving faster now. And faster. He warned me, but I'm still not ready.

My grip on his hand tightens again.

"Oh my god," I squeak. "This was a mistake. Think they'll let me off?"

"Only if you have a parachute."

I whip my head to look at him, only to end up face to face with him, our noses almost touching.

Our eyes lock, then his gaze flits to my lips.

My eyes widen in disbelief, and I brace myself for impact.

I think I'd like this kind.

He draws a breath, and my eyes drift to his neck, watching the muscles flex as he swallows hard.

Oh my.

My hand is starting to sweat again. For an entirely different reason.

I yank my hand away and wipe it on my pants, inhaling deeply as I lean back slightly. He does the same, but also doesn't fully shift back into his seat.

"We're flying now," he says softly.

I tear my gaze away from him and glance out the window. Clouds. I see fucking clouds. Below me. And the ground...we're thousands of feet above the earth. A chill rolls up my spine, and I yelp again.

"Everything okay here?" a flight attendant asks.

"I'm just a little nervous," I say, attempting to exude confidence I don't even slightly feel.

"She's never flown before," Mark whispers.

The flight attendant smiles as I glare at Mark.

"Could we maybe get some drinks?" he asks.

"Drinks? It's only nine in the morning," I protest.

And I swear, if he says 'it's five o'clock somewhere' I'll slug him and reexamine his nice-guy status.

"It's vacation. Time doesn't count on vacation."

I guess I'll let that slide. Mostly because I could definitely use something to take the edge off.

"Gin and tonic with lime, please."

Mark stifles a laugh. "And I'll have a whiskey and coke, lots of ice. Thanks."

I let out a breath and look down, realizing my hands are shaking. "Maybe I do need that drink."

"Hey, for what it's worth, I think you're doing pretty well on your first flight for someone who I'm assuming hates heights."

"That would be correct. I cry on Ferris wheels."

Again, he bites back a laugh. "Well then, you get extra points for making it this long without crying."

"Hey, it's still an option if I don't get my drink soon. Distract me."

His eyebrows go up. "Okay. Sure. Um..."

For the first time, he looks at me tentatively, then slowly pulls his baseball cap off. He looks at me again, and I have no idea what he wants.

Is he expecting me to compliment him on his stunning jawline? Because I absolutely could.

Does he think I'll chastise his messy hair? Maybe he's been with someone controlling before who nagged him about things like that.

I wonder if he has a girlfriend.

Why does that thought make my stomach lurch?

As I continue looking at him, I notice the remnants of what looks to be a black eye, but given the guy friends I've had over the years who have stood up for me, I know that a black eye doesn't make you a bad guy.

"Frannie?"

My eyes snap to his. *Shit.* I've been staring at him like an idiot.

"Hm?"

His eyes narrow for half a second, then a slow, easy smile spreads across his face.

"You wanted me to distract you."

"Right. So, go ahead."

"Okay... why don't you tell me where you're from?"

"This sounds like it's verging on small talk territory, but since we don't actually know each other, I'll allow. I'm from Manhattan, but I live in a small town upstate now."

"Where?" he asks, and I give him a skeptical look. Most small towns in New York aren't easily recognized by name. Hell, most people I meet assume that if you're from New York you live at the frigging Empire State Building. He smiles at my skepticism and says, "I live in Manhattan now, but I grew up near Watertown and have family throughout the state."

"Oh. Cool. I live in Ida. It's—"

"Along the Pennsylvania border, and it's home to a surprisingly good bunch of restaurants, maybe the best of which is Marion's Café, especially if you love chicken soup and grilled cheese."

He grins at my flared eyes and shocked expression.

"How did you..."

"My dad's family is from there. My grandparents, aunt and

uncle, and a few cousins still live there. It's like a second home to me."

I swallow hard at that revelation. I just so happened to end up sitting on a flight next to a guy who has ties to the same tiny town I live in? Plus, he's exceedingly nice, ridiculously good looking, and we seem to have a spark between us. What's that saying?

If it seems too good to be true, it probably is.

Seriously, where's the catch?

It's just a flight, Frannie. That's the catch. Whatever your connection or his ties to Ida, the likelihood of you ever seeing him again is next to nothing.

Focusing back on our conversation, I smile. "Marion's is phenomenal. I only live two blocks from the café and I'd probably have a lot more in my bank account if I didn't eat there so much. Not to mention the coffeehouse her daughter opened adjoining it. Oh my god, talk about incredible."

"My cousins have been saying that. I haven't made it there yet, but I'm hoping to get there soon."

We stare at each other for a beat, then I break the tension I feel forming and ask, "What do you do for a living?"

"Ah..." he hedges for a second, which surprises me, then says, "I work with numbers."

I laugh lightly. "I think that's what a lot of people do these days. But it's steady income and not too taxing of a job, right?"

He chuckles. "Something like that. Plus, I get a good amount of vacation time, which I like. What about you?"

I tell him about working for child protective services. Actually, I'm rambling about my job. Or maybe gushing. I bite my lip and laugh, rolling my eyes at myself. "In case you can't tell, I really love what I do. My boss had to force me to take a vacation. Something about it looking bad on them if an employee has too many unused vacation days."

"Sounds like you're on a much-needed vacation, then."

I nod. "Yeah. I probably could've started smaller. Or even

done a staycation. I'm happy just curling up in front of my window and reading a book."

"Is that what you do on your down time?" he asks.

"Yep."

"What's your genre of choice?"

"Oh. Hm. I'm not too picky, but I'm a mood reader. Mostly, I read contemporary fiction or romance on a daily basis, but I love fantasy, too, and I'll go on a binge of it sometimes and read an entire series in a weekend. Right now, though, I've been *deep* into a hockey romance hole and there's no coming out of it anytime soon." I pause for a breath, wondering if I'm coming off as crazy as I think I am in my head. "What about you?"

"Football," he says. Then he clears his throat. "I mean, I watch it."

I nod slowly. Sports is not my area of expertise. "Touchdowns. Tackles. And I'm out."

"You know nothing about football, do you?"

"Nope," I say cheerily.

"Well, I also like to read. Mystery. Sci-fi. Fantasy. I've been attempting to get through *Game of Thrones,* but..."

"Switch to the audiobooks," I tell him. "It's the only way I got through them, and I swear it made them so much easier. Of course, then the show had to go and ruin things and now..." I growl. "*GOT* and I are on a bit of a break."

He laughs out loud. "I feel that. Actually, I've gotten into the *Mistborn* series lately. I just finished the original trilogy, and—"

"Oh my god! I *love* that series."

"Yeah?"

I nod enthusiastically. I could discuss books all day, but I rarely have anyone to talk about them with.

The flight attendant returns with our drinks, and Mark and I settle into a deep discussion about the *Mistborn* universe that, for the first time, makes me forget I'm not on the ground.

CHAPTER THREE

Mark

I'VE NEVER HAD A MORE enjoyable flight. I didn't know what to expect when I sat down next to the woman who was rocking back and forth—and whispering Eminem lyrics?—but I'm glad I did. I'm glad I offered her my hand, offered to distract her. It turned into a great conversation with someone I feel a genuine connection to. The only thing I feel bad about is lying to her about my career—and last name. I used my mother's last name, since that's the name I'm traveling by to avoid attention.

If my grandfather could see me right now, he'd be giving me that shit-eating knowing smile of his.

I've never put much stock in instant love or even connection, despite the people in my family who have sworn to me that it happens. I mean, not that everyone in my family who has fallen in love has experienced love at first sight, but they definitely had instant connections. Hell, my cousin Rae held her husband's hand the day after she met him when they were five years old and she swears she knew then. Explains why it took them fifteen years to get together, but whatever. They aren't the only ones.

My dad saw my mom across campus at freshman orientation, and he says their eyes locked and it was a done deal from that moment on. They were married sophomore year and had my oldest brother, Mason, during their junior year.

Fucking insanity, if you ask me.

Maybe the only person in my family who doesn't swear by this instant connection nonsense is my grandmother. My grandfather will tell you it was love at first sight. Gram always rolls her eyes and says he annoyed her at first sight.

Then again, the look in her eyes whenever she says it makes me wonder if she enjoyed that annoyance.

Yet, with Frannie, I can't shake this feeling I have. Like I've known her forever, even though I just met her.

Yep, definitely insanity.

And I need to hold on to that feeling of insanity and disbelief about instant connection right now because we're about to part ways.

After the flight landed—which Frannie handled surprisingly well—we walked together off the plane, and I got her bag off the conveyor at baggage claim. She's headed to rent a car now, and I'm going to meet the associate from the private car company I rented from to get the keys.

"So, uh, thanks for putting up with my craziness. Hopefully, I didn't ruin your flight," Frannie says, scrunching her nose as she looks up at me.

"Definitely not ruined. It was fun. I hope I took your mind off the horrors of flying for a bit."

"You did. For sure."

We stare awkwardly at each other for a moment, and I consider giving her my number. It's not like it would be completely random. We hit it off. She lives in Ida, where I was planning to spend some time this spring. Then again, maybe this was supposed to be a chance meeting.

Grandpa would probably tell me it's fate.

I take a deep breath, remembering what this trip is supposed to be about—me, relaxing in a safe space. If it's fate, maybe we'll cross paths again in Ida. At Marion's. Who knows?

I gently squeeze her arm, then lean down and kiss her cheek.

"The flight was fun. Take care, Frannie."

"You too, Mark," she says with a smile.

With a lingering look, we turn and walk in opposite directions, but the weird, unsettling feeling in my gut nearly makes me turn around and jog back to her.

A brief meeting. That's all it was, I tell myself. But I'm not sure I believe it.

AFTER PICKING up the keys to the Subaru Ascent I'll be driving, I grabbed a latte. As I walk out of the building, I'm hit with a rush of warm air. Though it's a welcome change from the frigid temps in New York, it's an adjustment.

I walk down the sidewalk toward the parking lot where the car is waiting for me, when something else hits me—a familiar voice.

"Stupid... ridiculous... slashed car tires! Who does that? I'm *never* taking a vacation again!"

Walking up to the exasperated brown-haired woman, I smile. "Frannie?"

She jumps and turns toward me. "Mark? Oh. Hi."

I lift an eyebrow and bite back a smile. "Everything okay?"

She's leaning against a metal pole, phone in hand, looking stressed.

"Not exactly. Apparently, some asshole felt the need to slash the tires of all the cars for the rental service. The only other rental company is across town and an Uber ride there is..." She inhales sharply, looking at her phone. "Highway robbery. God damn it. Staycation next time."

"Well, where are you headed? Is your hotel nearby? I could drop you off."

She shakes her head and waves a hand, laughing in disdain. "That's the thing. My hotel *isn't* nearby. I've got a little over an hour drive to my destination. And unless you're about to tell me you're headed to a tiny town called…"

I start laughing like an idiot.

Yeah, okay. I get it.

"What?" she demands.

I don't know how it didn't come up on the plane. Probably because we went down a fantasy book rabbit hole.

"Anais Bay. Is that what you were about to say?"

Anais Bay, South Carolina is one of my favorite places in the world. It's the tiny town where my mother was born and spent the first few years of her life. We vacationed there every year when I was young because my great grandparents still lived there. After they passed, we still visited the town regularly, and it's a truly safe space. There are occasional tourists, but since it's nestled between Charleston and Hilton Head, it's much less busy than those popular destinations. But the town still has all the essentials. There's a grocery store, several seafood joints, a brewpub, and an incredible diner. Not to mention privacy. The resort I'm staying at is a friends-and-family type of place. You have to have a direct referral from someone who has stayed there before to reserve a room. Plus, if there's a town in the US where no one cares about football, it's Anais Bay. Fishing, snorkeling, and hiking rule life there.

Frannie's mouth drops open and she blinks a couple of times. "How did you know that?"

"It's where I'm headed, too. My mom's family is from there. None of them live there anymore, but I still go back often."

Her eyes widen. "Oh."

"You staying at the Evermore?" I ask.

She nods, eyes still huge.

"Good. Then you're riding with me. Once we're there, everything is within walking distance and the local taxi company is very reliable."

She looks around. "Are you sure?"

"Of course. We had plenty of fun on the flight. I'm sure we can survive an hour road trip."

Her face lights with a gorgeous smile that turns my insides to lava.

"Okay, then. Sounds good. Thank you."

"No problem."

She reaches for her suitcase, but I grab it.

"I've got it."

She looks up at me, eyes intense for a moment before she whispers, "Thanks."

"C'mon, it's this way."

As we walk toward the parking lot, my grandfather's words about fate roll through my mind.

"You don't get to control fate, sonny. It does what it wants, when it wants. And when it sneaks up and smacks you across the face, it always leaves a mark."

Score one for fate. And Gramps.

TWENTY MINUTES INTO OUR DRIVE, Frannie is tapping furiously on her phone and sighing.

"Texting your sister?" I ask.

She glances at me out of the corner of her eye, then shifts in her seat to look at me.

"Can you read my mind?"

I chuckle at that. "No. But I'm the youngest of four. Your exasperated sighs tell me you're talking to a sibling."

"Yeah." She looks back down at the phone, then rolls her eyes. "My little sister and my cousin—who is like my older sister. I made the mistake of mentioning you and..."

"Hm?"

"Now they're alternating between planning our wedding or my funeral. They can't seem to decide whether you're the love of my life or a serial killer about to murder me."

I consider asking her which she'd prefer me to be, but I worry that might take this conversation to a more serious place than either of us would like it to go.

"Whatever," she says with another sigh, then shoves her phone in her bag. "I'll deal with those maniacs later."

She turns and looks out the window, but her nose scrunches when all she sees is the highway.

Unfortunately, despite both Charleston and Anais Bay being directly on the coast, the drive takes us inland, so there aren't many good views.

"How about some music?" I ask.

"Sure. Unless you're one of those people into nothing but metal or gangster rap. Then I'll happily ride in silence."

"Not quite. Both of those are reserved for workout playlists. Even then, I'm not sure I have gangster rap. Whatever that is. I have a pretty eclectic taste. Mostly, I listen to playlists." I grab my phone from its holder and hold it out to her.

"Oh, I don't care then. Whatever."

"I'm not going to pick one while I'm driving, so you pick."

I use my thumb to unlock the screen, then hand the phone to her.

"I feel weird going through your phone, so I'm picking whichever one comes up first. Which is 'Daily Playlist #9?' What the hell kind of title is that? How do you know what's on it?"

"I play it."

She looks at me like I'm crazy, then pushes play and sets my phone back in the holder.

A second later, *Lose Yourself* by Eminem is playing, and

Frannie is laughing so hard she has tears streaming down her cheeks.

"Did you... do this... on purpose?" she asks, barely getting the words out between wheezes of laughter.

I glance at her for a second, then realization hits. "Wait. Were you singing this when I sat down next to you?"

"Humming it," she squeaks, still laughing. "I was thinking about how my *palms were sweaty*, then it got stuck in my head and now..."

"It's officially our song," I say dramatically.

"Yep. We'll play it at the wedding. Tell the grandkids about it." Her eyes dance and she laughs again before taking a deep breath and softly singing along with the song.

God help me, I'm infatuated with this girl. She's so real. Funny. Sweet with a hint of spice. Or maybe insanity. Either way, I like it. She's also both cute as a button and hot as hell. The way she can go from adorable to sultry in half a second messes with my mind—and body—in the best way. She keeps me on my toes. And if I was going to be with someone...

Oh, damn. My brain has already gone to that place. I look over at her again. She's still mouthing the words to the song as she twists her hair around her finger and smiles at me.

Fuck it.

I was planning on spending time alone on this trip, but now that sounds much less fun than spending time with her.

CHAPTER FOUR

Frannie

MUCH LIKE OUR flight to Charleston, our drive to Anais Bay was playful and relaxing.

Meeting Mark was unexpected, to say the least. What's even more unexpected is the way he lights me on fire. Heart, body, soul, all engulfed in flames.

I wasn't planning on hooking up on this trip mostly because I don't hook up. Ever. I'm either single and sitting alone with my books or in a super serious relationship. There's no in between. Since my last relationship ended two years ago—there was no bad blood, we just weren't right for each other—I've been in a serious relationship with my books.

One cute guy on a plane and I'm ready to drop my panties and fork over my heart.

Seriously, there's something wrong with me.

As we climb out of the car, I look around at the expansive Evermore resort. It's not as massive as something you'd find in a major tourist area, but it's big and beautiful and welcoming. There's something about this place that feels like home. Maybe that's why Mark enjoys coming here.

"C'mon," he says after grabbing our bags from the back of the car. "Check-in is this way."

He leads me up a small set of concrete stairs which open onto a covered concrete pad. It's open at the front and back, and beyond it is a stunning view of the ocean.

"Oh, wow," I breathe, stopping in place.

Mark stops and turns to me. "Beautiful, huh?"

"Mhm," I mutter, moving forward for a better look.

A second later, he's standing behind me, breath tickling my neck as he whispers, "Still wish you'd have taken a staycation?"

Gulping down the buildup of saliva in my throat, I take a deep breath, then turn back to him. "I think this might be worth it."

His vibrant smile melts me to my core.

"Well, we better check in so we can enjoy it."

He nods, and I follow him inside to the main desk.

Everything is open, bright, and airy with a beachy yet classy feel.

"Hi there. Mark Hainley. I'm checking in."

"Ah yes, Mark. It's good to see you again," the man at the desk says to him. Then he spots me. "I didn't realize you were traveling with someone."

"Oh, no. We're not, uh, together. We were just on the same flight, and I needed a ride and…" I clear my throat, realizing how ridiculous I sound. "Anyway, I'm checking in separately."

"Okay, then. Mark, you're in Room 315." The man looks over at me. "And you must be Frannie Baker."

"Yep. That's me."

"Wonderful. You're in Room 307." He slides a key card over to me.

"Thanks very much."

"Let me get someone to grab your bags."

"Oh, that's fine. I've got them," Mark says with a smile.

"Thanks," I say for what feels like the hundredth time today.

He grins at me. "No problem. Let's go."

I follow him toward the elevator, which opens as soon as he pushes the button. He still has my suitcase, and an awkward tension is settling between us. We've had a lot of fun together so far today, but where do we go from here? Assuming we'll both be here for a bit, does that mean we'll see each other again? Hang out? Wave awkwardly from across the room? That's what I'd end up doing.

The bell dings and the elevator doors open. Despite our conversations earlier, we're silent as a grave now, and I hate it. Silence is fine, but not when it's weird, uncertain silence like this.

"Here we are," Mark says, stopping in front of my hotel room. "307."

"Right. That's me."

He lets go of my suitcase and spins it toward me. As I grab the handle, our fingers brush, and we both look down at them.

Heat seeps into the tension surrounding us.

"Okay," Mark says, meeting my eyes. "Well, I'm in 315 if you need anything." He clears his throat.

"Sure. Thanks... for everything."

"You don't have to thank me, Frannie. I had a great time with you today."

"I had a good time, too."

We stare at each other and my skin crawls. I get second-hand embarrassment from awkward situations on TV shows. I'm not cut out for situations like this.

"So, I guess I'll see you around," I say.

"Yeah. Absolutely. Have a good night, Frannie."

"You too, Mark."

Without waiting for any further response, I shove the keycard in the slot and open the door, dragging my bags inside. I let the door shut behind me, then sigh as I lean against it.

But no sooner has my back touched the door, then there's a knock at it.

Spinning around, I push my bags to the side, then fling my door open to see Mark. His hazel eyes bore into me as I look up at him.

He shoves a hand through his hair and sighs. Then his lips pull into a half-smile and my core clenches in response.

"Look, I know this might sound crazy, but would you like to have dinner with me tonight? The restaurant here is incredible, and I... want to spend more time with you."

"Yes." The word flies out much faster than it should.

And his smile grows. "Perfect. I'll pick you up here at six."

"Can't wait." And I freaking can't. I cannot get enough of this guy.

"Great." He captures my hand in his and lightly brushes his thumb over my knuckles. "See you later, Frannie." He pulls me closer and kisses my cheek, then winks at me as he lets go of my hand.

"Later." I sound like a giggly middle schooler who just got asked out by her crush. But I can't help it.

He strolls down the hall, and I close the door, once again leaning against it. My hand comes to my cheek where his lips were, and I squeal to myself.

Then I realize I have to figure out what the hell to wear tonight because I didn't pack much that's date worthy.

First things first, I need to unpack.

Grabbing my oversized purse and my suitcase, I make my way into the room and for the first time, I actually notice what it looks like. It's got a king-size bed with crisp white bedding, a large oak dresser, a TV mounted on the wall above it, and a small refrigerator with a microwave above it. But my eyes are drawn to the sliding door at the far side of the room. I walk over and push the curtains aside, then pull the door open.

Oh my.

The door leads to a small balcony with a perfect view of the ocean. It's gorgeous.

Okay, maybe this vacation was a good idea after all.

Forcing myself away from the view, I head back inside and unpack my suitcase. Though I'll be here for ten days, I didn't bring too much. Mostly a bunch of tank tops, tees, shorts, and skirts. There are also a couple of swimsuits and three sundresses. I pull out the new one I bought last week, a pink floral dress with cap sleeves. Perfect for tonight. Beneath all my clothes are my shoes. I wore sneakers for the plane ride and packed cheap flip-flops, nice Roman-style sandals, and a pair of cream-colored braided wedges. I set those aside to wear with my dress tonight.

Glancing at the time, I see it's almost one o'clock. Mark and I stopped at a drive through for burgers on the way here, so I'm not hungry. I am exhausted, though. Maybe I'll rest for a bit, then explore the resort before I get ready for my date tonight.

Date?

I guess that's what it is. That's sure what it seems like.

I kick my shoes off, then peel off my socks. A shower is definitely in order for tonight.

Grabbing my bag, I pull both my phone and my Kindle out, only for my phone to vibrate as I do. Looking at it, I see I have a plethora of missed texts in my group chat with Hallie and Kennedy. And a missed video chat request. Whoops.

Instead of reading all the texts they've sent me, I scroll down and look at the last few.

> **KENNEDY**
>
> You should be there by now!
>
> **HALLIE**
>
> If Frannie is lying in a shallow grave and the killer is reading this... just know, I will find you.
>
> **KENNEDY**
>
> If you don't answer in the next five minutes, I'm calling the police. Maybe the FBI.

HALLIE

And Jack Bauer!

Sighing, I shake my head. Thankfully, I haven't met Kennedy's deadline yet.

I click on the button to video chat with them and wait for their answer.

"Oh! Look, Kend! She's alive," Hallie says as she and Kennedy pop up on the screen in individual chat bubbles.

Kennedy tilts her head back and forth. "And I don't see any signs of being held against her will."

"I'm not being held against my will. I'm here in my hotel room, alone." I get up and spin the camera so they can see a full view before sitting back down on the bed. "See? All good. So no need to go all *Taken* or contact Kiefer Sutherland's alter ego. 'Kay?"

"I suppose," Kennedy says.

"So, where's the hottie? Is he there? Give me a glimpse!" Hallie says as Kennedy rolls her eyes.

"He's not here. I just told you I'm alone. He dropped me off at my room."

"Ooh, walked you to your room, huh?" Hallie asks.

"Yes."

"Did he carry your bags too?" Kennedy asks.

"He rolled my suitcase behind him."

"Ooh. We're definitely leaning toward soul mates now," Hallie says as Kennedy nods in agreement.

Why these two are so obsessed with the idea is beyond me. Hallie hates the idea of falling in love. I don't know why. Our parents are still married, as are most of the important people in our lives, but she's totally against falling in love. But only for herself, apparently. And Kennedy has zero room to talk. If she wants to obsess over a love story, she should grow some ovaries and *finally* make a move on her best friend Devon. They've been blatantly in love with each other for years, they're just too dumb to see it.

Whatever. They need to let this go.

"Would you stop with that? I don't need that kind of pressure. Especially before—" I clamp my mouth shut, but it's too late.

"Before what?" Kennedy asks.

"Nothing."

"Before. What?" Hallie demands.

Dragging my hand over my face, I know there's no escaping this. I flip my hair back and cooly say, "My date with Mark."

Hallie screeches and Kennedy grabs her phone, bringing it closer to her face so all I see are her wide eyes.

"A date, huh? You know if you needed to get laid this badly, you didn't need to go to a whole new state to do it," Kennedy says.

"Will you shut up? I was not planning this. Not at all. But we have a connection... I don't know if it'll turn into more. Maybe we'll end up being best friends. Who knows? All I know is we're having dinner tonight. And until then, I want to enjoy my vacation. So, shut up and let me do that."

"Wow, she really likes him," Kennedy says to Hallie, as they both fawn over whatever it is that's happening between Mark and me.

"Definitely," Hallie agrees. "At least this means we get to plan a wedding and not a funeral."

"And on that lovely note, have fun finding my wedding dress. I'm going to check out the beach."

"Send lots of pictures!" Kennedy says.

"Yes. And have fun!" Hallie commands.

"I will. Love you both."

"Love you," they both say, then the call ends.

Hallelujah.

The sunlight streaming in from the window grabs my attention, and I walk back over to the sliding door and pull it open, stepping out onto the balcony.

This is my personal paradise for the next ten days.

I snap a quick picture, then send it to Hallie, Kennedy, my boss—who texted and wished me a safe trip—and my friend who recommended this place to me.

Though I was going to lie down and rest or read, the beach is calling my name. After putting my favorite purple bikini on and lathering up with sunscreen, I grab a beach towel from the rack in the bathroom and head down to the beach.

CHAPTER FIVE

Mark

THIS VACATION IS GOING nothing like I planned, and it's only the first day. That's not a complaint. Meeting Frannie upended my plans in the best possible way. Minus the fact that I can't get her out of my mind.

And I *need* her out of my mind right now.

Do not jack off to the mental image of Frannie.

Don't.

Fuck.

I thrust my cock through my fist as I brace the shower wall with my other hand. Water streams over me as steam fills the room.

I try to think about the last porno I watched. The tits on that jersey chaser who nearly accosted Ackley and me after we lost the game. She was sure as shit determined to get one of us off.

Nothing is working. My mind is blank except for the image of Frannie in that purple bikini on the beach earlier. I saw her from a distance and watched shamelessly as she strolled down the beach, her perfectly round ass peeking out of her bikini bottoms. I thought about walking over to her, spending more time with her, but more than anything, I want to enjoy our date, and figured letting more tension build would be good.

Except that tension went straight to my dick as I imagined running my hands over her soft stomach, sucking the skin of her neck into my mouth, squeezing that gorgeous ass.

I grunt as I work my hand faster. There's no getting out of it now. I can't get Frannie off my mind, and I'm about to...

"Oh fuck," I groan, as my cum hits the shower wall.

Panting, I tightly close my eyes.

At least I got some of those pent-up feelings out before my date with her, so I'm not sporting a semi that would be all too visible through my linen shorts.

Flashing my eyes open, I look down at my dick, issuing a silent command to calm the hell down and stay that way. I actually like this girl, and I'd rather not scare her off.

Turning off the water, I climb out of the shower and towel off, then throw on my boxers and some exercise shorts. Standing in front of the sink, I lean forward and look into the large mirror, running a hand over my cheek.

To shave or not to shave? I forget if stubble is supposed to be sexy or not. My sister, Andrea, gave me a whole lecture about it, then my cousins, Dani, Olivia, Rae, and Sarah, chimed in. I quickly tuned out after that, which is probably why I don't remember.

I grab my phone off the counter and prop it against the wall, then video call the one person who will give me the answer to my shaving dilemma.

The first thing I see when the call goes through are two massive black pecs and the upper part of Hardy's eight-pack.

"Dude. Camera angle."

"Sorry, my man." He adjusts the camera and grins at me. "How's vacation?"

"It's good. I have a dumb question for you."

"My favorite kind."

"Hey! Who's that?" Ackley calls from the background. The two live in neighboring condos and spend an inordinate amount of time together. Hell, they can finish each other's sentences.

"Markie Mark."

"Oh, god. How many times do I need to tell you not to call me that?"

"At least a hundred more," Hardy replies as Ackley enters the frame as well.

"What's up? How's vacation? How's the beach? Can you send me a picture?"

"Are you aware that you also have the money and time to take a beach vacation yourself? Look, I don't have much time, and I need Hardy to answer a question."

"Hit me with it."

"Stubble or no stubble?"

"Uh. What?" Ackley asks.

"Really? You're going to make me say it again?" I ask.

Hardy strokes his chin. "I need context."

"Cont... fuck you. You don't need any context to answer me about whether stubble is sexy or not."

Hardy and Ackley exchange a glance as I wallow in regret over making this stupid call.

"If you want an answer from me, I most certainly need *context.*"

Asshole.

"Fine," I huff. "I have a date tonight."

"Woo, buddy! Yes. Markie Mark is finally about to get laid. It's about damn time, dude."

Ackley plops down on the couch next to Hardy as I groan. And question why I'm friends with them. I should've called Dani. Of all my cousins, she's the most no-bullshit and would've given me an answer without an inquisition.

"I thought you were anti-hookup," Ackley says.

"I'm not anti-hookup. I'm anti-jersey chasers. Don't get me wrong, all the respect. They know what they want and they have the proverbial balls to go after it, but I want something *more* than that."

"And this girl is more? Did you bring her with you? Find an ex or something?" Hardy asks.

"No. I met her on the plane. We have a lot in common. She's sweet. Look, I promise to call you and gush about the date tomorrow and you can swoon onto your fainting couches, but for now, please, just tell me, yes or no stubble?"

"Yes," Hardy says, at the same time Ackley says, "No."

Hardy and Ackley stare at each other.

"Christ, you two are useless. Why did I call you?"

"To be fair, you called *me,*" Hardy points out. "Because I know women."

"To Mark's earlier point, you know the jersey chasers. They'll tell you whatever you want to hear if you let them suck your dick."

Hardy stares at Ackley, dumbfounded.

Ackley grins at me. "No stubble, man. Girls like that boyish look."

I stare at my phone in disbelief. "Okay, that's it. You're both fired."

Hardy strokes his beard. "Maybe you need to grow that stubble out."

"I've gotta go figure out what to do with my face since you two are wildly unhelpful."

"Hey, call us tomorrow!" Ackley says.

"I second that. I want to hear about this girl. Blonde? Brunette? Curvy?"

"Goodbye."

I end the call to the sound of their laughter. *Assholes.*

Then I pick up my phone and do what I should've done in the first place.

> I have one minute to decide this. Stubble or
> no stubble for my date tonight?

Thankfully, Dani responds quickly.

DANI

Oh. A date. Nice. Well, really, it's more about
what she likes, but if you don't know that, go
with what you like. Whatever you feel most
confident with. I can't fully decide that for you,
but when I think about the most authentic
version of you, it includes stubble. Mostly
because you hate routine shaving, but beards
bug you.

Damn it. How did she make it that easy?

> I love you. And I owe you dinner whenever I'm
> in Ida next.

DANI

I'll always take dinner with you. Have fun on
your date! Love ya cuz!

Stubble decision made—because she's right. I hate shaving regu-larly enough to have a baby face but also feel insanely itchy when I have a beard—I walk out to the bedroom and grab my clothes for tonight.

I chose a comfortable beachy feel—dark tan linen shorts with a light blue linen button-down and light brown loafers.

After getting dressed, I go back to the bathroom and grab my mousse, messing with my hair until it has that sexily mussed look that's supposed to make it seem like I just rolled out of bed but still look sexy as fuck. Then I grab my favorite cologne—it's light and subtle—spritz some next to me, and walk through it.

Checking the time, I see I have ten minutes until I need to pick up Frannie. One last thought occurs to me, so I grab my wallet and keys and head out the door.

WHEN WAS the last time I went on a date? Not the rare occasion of picking a girl up to meet both of our needs for the night—which I haven't done much since I joined the New York Bandits. Not hanging out—and subsequently hooking up with— an ex, which, I must admit, tends to be my go-to. I'm on good terms with most of them, and for my high school ones, if we're both single in the same location, we're good to go. Again, I haven't used that much in the last couple of years.

When you end up in the public eye, people want more from you by nature. You're a prize. Something to brag about, show off, or get something from. Not everyone, but plenty of people are like that, and the ones willing to go home with you for a night? They're the ones most likely to be.

The last actual date I went on must have been during freshman year of college. That was the last time I had a girlfriend. The relationship fizzled out after a month of practice and the grueling football schedule at a Division I school. I didn't bother trying after that. In college, finding a girl who wanted to hook up was as simple as wearing my football hoodie—for the first year. After that, all I had to do was enter the room. Sorority and frat parties were guaranteed hookup nights, and I took full advantage. I was careful, clear about my intentions, and never did anything when either of us was too drunk, but while I was Mr. Popular on campus, I wasn't anywhere else, so I didn't mind sowing my wild oats as the saying goes.

I sowed a lot.

Then I worked out.

Class.

Practice.

Repeat.

Now?

Work out.

Practice.

Go home alone and get acquainted with my hand.

Repeat.

I may live and breathe football, but that doesn't mean I don't want more for my life one day.

And now that I've sufficiently psyched myself out, I'm standing outside Frannie's hotel room, ready to go on a date for the first time in five years.

Cool.

With a deep breath, I raise my hand and knock on the door.

A moment later it swings open and any fear I had melts away.

Her tinted pink lips curve into a smile, but I only see them for a moment as my eyes trail down her body. Her long light brown hair is swept behind her shoulders, and she's wearing a pink and white dress that shows off her neckline and hugs the curve of her perfect tits before flaring out below the waist. It hits at her mid-thigh, and paired with the tall wedges she's wearing, her legs look a damn mile long.

She clears her throat and my eyes snap back to hers.

"Sorry," I say with a grin, indicating that I'm not sorry at all.

She bites her lip in response, and I'm extra grateful I beat one off earlier. If I make it through this date without getting a hard-on, it'll be a fucking miracle.

"These are for you," I finally say, extending the flowers I got at the resort gift shop. They're decent for being pre-cut and already in a vase. It's a small bouquet of local wildflowers, but hopefully, it'll do the trick.

"Thank you. They're beautiful."

"So are you."

She cocks an eyebrow and looks me over. "If you mean it, that's sweet. But don't use lines on me. I don't need any kind of commitment, but I don't want to play games, either."

"You're not a game to me, Frannie. And of course I meant it. I was vocalizing what I thought my eyes said pretty clearly when you opened the door."

Her cheeks tinge pink, but she smiles. "Good answer." She sets the vase to the side, then grabs her bag. Leaning in toward me, she whispers, "For the record, you look hot as hell." She winks at me and steps into the hall, closing the door behind her. "Shall we?"

CHAPTER SIX

Frannie

"THIS MENU…" I let out a dreamy sigh. "I could order one of everything. It all sounds so good. And I'm starving. Gah! How do I pick?"

Mark chuckles. "Well, the good news is, you have eight more nights after this to try things, right?"

I bob my head up and down, but I'm still staring at the menu. Lobster mac and cheese or shrimp scampi? Maybe surf and turf? Crab cakes? How do I pick?

Mark puts his hand on the menu, lowering it.

"What's your favorite food?" he asks.

"Ever?"

"Okay, something from your top five."

"Lobster ravioli," I say, looking at the item listed on the menu.

"There you go. Start there."

"Oh, I'm starting with the crab dip and crostini appetizer."

"Then you're sharing, because that's fucking incredible. My mouth is watering now. I've missed this place."

A waiter walks up and asks for our drink orders.

I order zinfandel and water. Mark also orders water in addition to a bottle of IPA from a local brewery.

"Would you like me to bring a bottle, Miss?" the waiter asks.

"Oh. No, thank you. Just the glass."

Since we've both decided, we give him our meal orders as well, with Mark choosing a steak and pasta combo with a crab cake appetizer.

"Funny, I thought you were sharing my appetizer," I say as the waiter leaves.

"I am. You share your crab dip, I share my crab cakes, and we both go home happy. By the way, feel free to have another glass of wine if you like. Money's no object tonight."

"You don't have to pay," I say.

He pins me with a look that says he is absolutely paying and I better not fight him about it.

"Fine. Either way, no second glass of wine for me. If I drink two, I lose all rational decision-making skills, then suddenly I'm drinking three or four or five."

He smiles and nods. "Okay then, no second glass of wine for you. Should I plan on snatching it from your hand if you order one when I'm not looking?"

I smile at that. "Good, you passed the test."

"The test?"

"The number of dates I've been on where I said something similar and was told 'Oh, I better get you that second glass, then' in an extremely pervy way is more than I'd like to admit."

Without missing a beat, he says, "Then you've been dating boys, not men. *Men* don't need to get a woman drunk. In fact, they should want her to be clear-headed so she remembers every perfect detail." A sly smile crosses his lips, and *damn*. That is some sexy shit. I'm not sure if it's a line or not, and I don't really care.

"Good answer." My eyes drift over his shoulder to the dark ocean. Back home, I'm used to the sun setting early this time of year. It's cold, and it seems like the sun *should* set early. Here, when it's still warm outside, the sun setting so early seems like a waste. "This place is beautiful."

"It is. What made you choose Anais Bay for your big vacation?"

I shrug. "A friend recommended it. I'd always wanted to spend time at a nice beach resort but had no desire to go to Florida or Mexico or the Caribbean, so this seemed like a good place. You know, until I got on the plane. You said you come here a lot, right?"

He nods. "Yeah. It feels less like going on vacation and more like visiting a hometown in some ways. It's comforting."

"Lots of memories here?"

"Oh yeah. As a family, we came here every year until my sister graduated from college a few years ago. After that, it became more individual trips. I came with my older brother and his wife a couple of times. What about you? Did you take a lot of family vacations?"

"Not big ones. We did more day trips. We did drive to Disney when I was thirteen. My parents and my aunt and uncle decided to do a combined trip."

"Close knit family?"

I chuckle at that. "My dad's brother and my mom's sister are married. That's how my parents met. When we were young, our dads bought a duplex. My aunt, uncle, and cousin lived on one side, and we lived on the other. It felt kind of like growing up in a little club."

"I get that. My uncle's kids are a lot younger than me, but they live on the same property as my parents. There's also a guesthouse on the property for the rest of my dad's family. We're all pretty close."

"That's awesome. There's something special about having close relationships with your family. Not everyone does." Hurt fills my chest as I say the words. I wish my mother's lies didn't still cause me pain, but that sort of betrayal doesn't just fade away.

Mark's fingers brush my hand, drawing my focus back to him. His curly auburn hair is tousled perfectly, and his handsome face is dotted with stubble. He has an easy sexiness about him. Like it exudes from somewhere inside him. Calm, confident, happy... himself. Most people aren't authentic or comfortable with who they are. Maybe because they don't know who they are. I'm proud of the work I've done on myself. I know who I am, what I want, what I'll tolerate, and what I won't.

"Okay?" Mark asks, head tilted to the side.

A smile forms as his fingers curl around mine. "I'm perfect."

The waiter returns and sets our drinks down, along with some fresh bread and butter.

"Absolutely perfect."

"YOU WENT CLIFF JUMPING? I'm sorry. I don't believe it. Not for a second." Mark shakes his head.

"I swear!"

"Coming from the woman who nearly cried on the plane this morning, and, by your own admission, cries on Ferris wheels."

"Okay, so maybe Kennedy and Hallie each took one of my hands and dragged me to the edge while I was crying. But I still did it."

He throws his head back, laughing.

God, that throat. The way his Adam's apple bobs as he swallows. I want to lick him.

What is wrong with me?

I'm never like this on a date.

He tightens his grip on my hand—which he hasn't let go of for longer than a few minutes all night.

I'm smitten.

Gah. Why am I using that word? I sound like I'm from the 1930s.

"That sounds more like it," he says.

"It was traumatizing, but exhilarating. I'm glad I did it."

"But would you do it again?"

"Only with the right person," I tell him, eyes locked on his.

When a waiter walks by with a tray of desserts, I glance down at the empty table in front of us. The bill has been paid, but we're still sitting here. I check my phone and my eyes widen.

"Oh my gosh. Do you realize we've been sitting here for three hours?"

His eyes widen. "No. It... didn't feel like that long." He looks around. "We should probably let them have the table. How about a walk on the beach?"

"I'd love that."

He stands up and extends his hand to me. I take it and stand, then hand in hand we walk down the stairs from the large stone patio where we were eating to the beach.

Even at night, the view is stunning.

We stop and look out at the stars over the water.

"This is beautiful. Tonight has been amazing. Especially the food."

He lets out an easy laugh. "Well, I know the way to your heart now. I've never seen anyone look at a chocolate torte the way you did tonight."

I glance up at him. "And how did I look at it?"

He sweeps one hand up the side of my face, fingers threading my hair. "Like nothing could make you happier."

My breath hitches in my throat as his eyes lock on mine.

Slowly, so fucking slowly, he lowers his lips to mine and presses a gentle kiss against them.

A chill rolls over me as the sparks between us flare, flying everywhere.

Our kiss is easy, not urgent or frantic, but fully about the pleasure of our lips touching.

When his soft lips lift off mine, I'm left aching for more. More kissing, more intensity, more of him.

"I had a great time tonight," he says softly.

"So did I."

"Does that mean we can do it again tomorrow?"

"I'd love that."

Hallie, Kennedy, my boss, and well, everyone else were right. I need to take vacations more often. Clearly, I've been missing out on something magical. No dates back home, but one vacation and I've got a second date with a hot-as-sin man.

We walk down the beach to the edge of the resort, then turn and head back to the resort. Our walk is quiet with only occasional conversation.

By the time we get back to the resort, tension is brewing between us. Our kiss didn't satiate either of us, it made us ravenous for more.

In the elevator, he brushes his thumb over my hand and pulls me closer to him, hazel eyes gleaming. My chest tightens and I swallow hard. As I stare up at him, my lips part. But as his head dips toward mine, the elevator doors open.

"That's us," Mark says thickly.

His grip on my hand tightens as he leads me off the elevator and toward my room.

When we get to my door, our eyes meet again.

My heartbeat ticks up as he licks his lips.

For a moment, we stare at each other. No words. Nothing. Just a lingering, tension-filled look until we can't take it anymore.

He dips his head down at the same time I reach up and grab the back of his neck. Our lips collide with a sharp jolt of electricity, and unlike on the beach, this kiss is intense, frantic, begging for more. I part my lips immediately, inviting him inside, and he doesn't waste a second before gliding his tongue into my mouth.

His demanding tongue strokes mine, twisting around it, pushing against it, deepening our kiss with each forceful movement.

Wrapping an arm around my back, he moves closer, pressing me against the door of my room. The pressure of his lips against mine is so strong I can barely breathe, and I give in. My body melts against the door as I try to match the voraciousness of his kisses while getting lost in them at the same time.

I run my hand down his chest to his stomach, feeling the taut abs beneath his shirt.

A noise, somewhere between a whimper and a moan, slips from my mouth and urges him on. I fist his shirt, every nerve ending in my body lighting up.

As I wonder what's going to happen next, he rips his lips from mine and stares at me, panting heavily.

My breaths are just as rough as his, but that doesn't stop the desire flowing between us. His eyes scan my face and then...

Crash.

Our mouths meet again.

This kiss is softer but still powerful, easing us out of the depths and back to reality. The pressure lessens and millimeter by millimeter he lifts his lips off mine, his hazel eyes intense as he takes me in.

He kisses my cheek, then says, "Tomorrow."

"Tomorrow," I agree.

There's that heart stopping half-smile. "Good. Have a good night, Frannie."

"Goodnight, Mark."

He takes a step back, but doesn't walk away as I open my door. I give one last wave as I step inside, then close the door behind me. Pressing onto my toes, I look through the peephole and watch as Mark struts away.

Back on flat feet, I lean against the door, breathless, as I gently touch my lips. I can still feel his lips on mine, and I won't forget it any time soon.

I don't care what happens from here. This is officially the best vacation ever.

CHAPTER SEVEN
MONDAY

Frannie

MORNING SUNLIGHT PEEKS around the edge of the curtains as I pull the pillow I'm holding closer and yank the covers up farther. Sun, warmth, the beach... it's all beautiful. But it'll still be beautiful in another hour.

I've trained myself to get up early for my job, but on the weekends, I sleep until at least nine. Preferably ten. Mornings and I are not BFFs. We've made a grudging agreement to tolerate each other, but whenever we can avoid each other, we do.

Snuggling deeper in the cozy nest I've built myself, I've nearly drifted off again when there's a knock at the door.

Why?

Maybe I forgot to put up the "Do Not Disturb" sign. They should have one that reads "until noon."

Another knock, and I groan.

Forcing myself upright, I throw off my blankets and make my

way to the door. When I swing it open, I'm greeted with Mark's stupidly charming face.

"Mark? What are you doing here? What time is it?" I resist the urge to rub my eyes.

"Just before nine," he says.

I squint at him. "Before nine? You do realize this is vacation, right?"

He chuckles, a smile lighting up his face. "I'm up at five most days. Seven is sleeping in for me."

Oh, god. He's a morning person.

"You know what, that kiss last night was hot, but if you're an energetic morning person, I don't think this is going to work."

His eyebrows go up and he looks at me, amused.

"What if I bribe you with some delicious food?"

My eyes meet his, and I stare at him for a beat. "You have my attention."

"The diner in town makes the best pancakes you'll ever taste, but that's nothing compared to their homemade bagels and the farm fresh bacon and eggs they cook up. Or their homemade corned beef hash. Top it all off with real maple syrup and fresh-squeezed orange juice..."

My eyes narrow to slits as I take it all in. That sounds delicious, even if my right eye is twitching because it doesn't want to be open yet. Then my stomach rumbles. *Fine, decision made.* I step back, opening the door all the way. "Okay, you may enter." As I walk into the room, I ask, "How's the coffee at the diner?"

"Not the best, but there's a coffee place here at the resort. They use local coffee and espresso. We can stop there first."

I stop and stretch, yawning big. *Definitely going to need coffee.*

Mark chokes on a breath, and for the first time, I realize what I'm wearing. Or barely wearing. V-cut tank that is sitting low on my boobs, nipples absolutely poking through it, and a pair of sleep shorts that are from my teen years and don't fit my adult ass all that well.

Like the gentleman he's proven himself to be, he looks away, but it's clear I'm torturing him.

Getting me up before nine is torturing me, so payback's fair game.

Pretending I haven't noticed him looking at me, I strut over to the dresser, open the drawer, and bend over more than I need to so my ass is on full display.

"I need to get ready first."

"I'll wait for you on the balcony," he says, voice cracking like a preteen boy. "The beach is beautiful this morning."

After grabbing clothes, I stand up and look at him, one eyebrow cocked. "If you say so."

Then I walk into the bathroom, swaying my hips as I go.

That's what he gets for waking me up early.

DESPITE MARK'S massive character flaw of being an early riser, the coffee at the resort was delicious and energized me, and the breakfast was even better than he promised, so I've decided to give him a pass.

Plus, I got to see a bit of the town—the main street, at least. It's adorable with little shops scattered everywhere. In the middle of the street, the road widens to go around a large fountain, which Mark and I tossed pennies into after breakfast. Idyllic doesn't even begin to describe this place. It gives me Stars Hollow vibes but with a more laid-back feel.

For being so close to Charleston, it seems like a hidden gem. There are some tourists, clearly enough to support the local businesses, but not so many that it has lost its small town charm.

After breakfast, we took the three-block walk back to the resort, and we've been relaxing on the beach ever since. There's a warm snap right now, and it's been around eighty each day we've been here, which is perfect beach weather.

We're on a blanket partially shaded by a beach umbrella. While I'm sitting up enjoying the sun, Mark's lying next to me in the shade, propped up on one elbow, shirtless. He looks like he belongs in a hot-men-on-the-beach calendar.

"Favorite color?" he asks.

We've been playing twenty questions as a way to get to know each other better. Though we talked about our families and our love of fantasy books and my epic fear of heights—for which Mark told me about his fear of snakes—yesterday, and then got deeply acquainted with each other's mouths, we still don't actually know all that much about each other.

"Coral," I say.

"Lighter or more orange-y?" he asks, to which I raise my eyebrows.

He laughs. "My cousin is an interior designer. Whether I want to or not, I know about color palettes. She was so frustrated with me that all I cared about were dark tones. 'You need some color in your life, Mark!' Don't get me wrong, I like color just fine, but my apartment is very modern, and I wanted a style that went with that."

"That's great," I say with a laugh. "So, what's *your* favorite color?"

"Ocean blue." But when I look at him, I realize he's not looking at the ocean. He's looking at me. At *my* blue eyes.

"That's a good color," I say, voice choppy.

A cheeky grin grows, and slowly, he sits up, eyes smoldering. He inches closer, then rolls over the top of me, brushing my hair away from my face as he looks into my eyes.

"It is a good color."

Then his lips are on mine. It's a slow, drawn-out kiss. His tongue lazily sweeps my mouth. No urgency, just fun, playful kisses.

He threads his fingers through my hair as I drag mine over the muscles of his shoulders.

He groans and my core clenches.

No one has ever turned me on like this before. Last night, after our kiss, I slid into bed and immediately my hand was between my legs as I imagined his lips on mine again. And maybe I imagined what it would've felt like for his hand to trail down my stomach, for his finger to dip inside me.

Shit, now I'm thinking about that all over again.

Oh. And I think he is, too. For the first time, I feel something hard pressing against my thigh.

"Mark," I whisper.

He lifts his lips off mine. "Sorry." His smirk says he isn't, but I don't want him to be.

"Don't be. But out here might not be the best place for that."

"Right," He agrees, pushing onto his knees. "I think my back was already getting sunburned, too."

"Yeah, the midday sun isn't as enjoyable."

"What were you planning on doing with your afternoons on this trip?"

"Probably swimming in the indoor pool or reading. Definitely reading," I say with a laugh.

"Well, I skipped my run this morning because I wanted to take you to breakfast."

Aw. Also, unnecessary.

"If you want to go read," he continues. "I'll go for a run and then meet you in your room after?"

"You're going to run in this heat?"

He laughs. "I can run in pretty much any weather."

"Ooh. Two strikes. Morning person and a runner?" I make a tsk noise with my tongue.

"Not a fan of running?"

"Not so much. The only time you'll find me running is when I'm pissed. Nothing gets me outside or on a treadmill faster than needing to burn some anger off. Otherwise, I'm more of a yoga and Pilates girl. And I like biking, both stationary and actual."

"Good to know. This is a great place for bikes. They rent them here at the resort. Maybe we could do that at some point."

"That would be great."

He grabs my hands and pulls me upright, then kisses my cheek. "All right then, a run for me while you read, then I'll come to your room after?"

"Sounds perfect. For the record, don't ever feel like you need to skip your run for me. Just come wake me up after."

"Deal," he says, giving me a quick kiss before jogging toward the resort as I enjoy the view of his tight ass until he's out of sight.

OH MY GOD. This book has me in a chokehold. That might be hockey romances in general, but this one is *so* good.

Hallie recommended it, so I actually bought a physical copy when it was on sale a couple of months ago. Since I got back to my room, I've been holed up in bed reading. Did I take my book into the bathroom with me when I had to pee? Yes.

And the further I get in, the harder I binge. I'm hitting the climactic point now, and I'm stress sweating for the characters. I know the thing that messes everything up is coming.

When there's a knock at the door, I climb out of bed, then walk over to it, nose still buried in a book. Of all the Disney princesses, I'm *definitely* Belle.

Pulling the door open, I give Mark a cursory glance.

"Hi. Come on in. I'm right at the intense climactic part of the book, and I'm not stopping, so you're welcome to hang out. But if there's some sort of zombie apocalypse happening, I'm going to need you to barricade the door." I look up at him again for half a second. "And I might use you as a meat shield."

He stifles a laugh, then kisses my cheek. "No worries. I brought my Kindle."

"Good." Without another word, I return to the bed.

Mark sits down next to me, and I completely lose myself in the book again. From breaking up for all the wrong reasons to coming back together to a perfect happily ever after, I'm so absorbed I lose track of time or what's going on around me.

When I finally finish, I set the book down, blinking a few times. *Book hangover initiated.*

After a few deep breaths, I glance at my phone and realize I binge read for four hours straight. And Mark has been sitting here with me for over an hour. Not once did he get annoyed with me or try to drag my attention back to him, he just let me read. His hand is on my thigh, but not in an attention-grabbing sort of way, just because he wants to touch me.

I've known him for a day, and yet he's shown a greater understanding of me than guys I dated for months. He was content to sit here with me, let me read, yet still enjoy my presence and a simple physical connection.

Is he a unicorn?

"You're staring at me," he says, eyes not lifting from his Kindle.

"Are you at an intense moment?" I ask.

He looks up and meets my gaze. "No."

"Good." I shove the Kindle to the side and climb onto his lap, kissing him hungrily. Greedy, fervent kisses as I run my hands through his hair and twist my tongue against his.

It doesn't take him long to catch up. He wraps his arms around my back and pulls me closer, deepening our kiss and adding fuel to the flames of desire already burning for him.

"Frannie," he groans against my mouth, causing me to pull away and look at him.

In a fluid motion, he rolls us over so we're resting face to face on our sides.

"Can I?" he rasps, running his hand over the hem of my shirt.

With a hard swallow, I nod.

This is crazy. I never hook up with guys I just met, but somehow it feels like I've known Mark forever.

He pulls my shirt off and tosses it onto the floor, then leans back to look at me.

"You're beautiful. I'm not sure I've said that to you yet, but I've thought it so many times. You're fucking stunning." He traces the lace at the edge of my bra, causing goosebumps to prickle.

"I don't know if you've said it to me, but your eyes said it this morning."

"That fucking tank top. And those shorts should be illegal. Jesus, Frannie. I had to have a serious conversation with my dick about behaving himself."

"And what about now?" I ask, biting my lip as I graze my hand over his crotch.

He shudders. "He doesn't want to behave anymore."

Leaning forward, I kiss his neck. "Maybe he doesn't need to."

Mark stares at me for a beat, then crushes his mouth against mine in another frantic kiss. His hand roams over my back, then down to my ass. With one hand, I reach behind my back and unclasp my bra, then shimmy out of it.

Not missing a beat, Mark brings his other hand up to my chest and cups my breast, running the rough pad of his thumb over my nipple and simultaneously creating a tingling, throbbing feeling between my legs.

Oh, god. I've never been this hot for someone before.

His thumb circles my nipple as I slide my hands under his shirt and up his back, aching to feel the warmth of his skin against mine, to be pinned beneath him, for our sweaty, writhing bodies to connect in every way.

"Mark," I breathe against his lips. "I—"

A loud, blaring noise cuts me off.

"What is that?" I ask loudly.

Mark sits up and looks around, then his eyes get big. "Fire alarm."

"Fire alarm?" I choke out.

"Yes. Get up."

"I'm not wearing a shirt." And my heart is racing. I feel sick to my stomach.

Mark's eyes dart over me, then he yanks his shirt off, pulls it over my head and pushes my arms through the sleeves.

"We need to go. Take my hand. I'm going to get us out of here safely."

I nod and take his outstretched hand as he leads me to the door, grabbing my purse and chucking my key card in it on the way out.

I swear, I'm not usually this useless, but fires trigger me.

Keeping my eyes half-closed, I let Mark lead me, trying to take deep breaths as we go.

When we get to the stairwell, I open my eyes slightly, but Mark is still directing my movements as I try not to let the sounds of people filling the space around us scare me more.

Once we get to the main floor, staff directs us to the doors leading onto the patio.

With a death grip on my hand, Mark leads me across the massive patio and down to the beach. He loosens his grip and intertwines our fingers as he stares up at the building, but I don't look. My eyes are tightly shut.

"Frannie? You're shaking. Are you okay?"

He pulls my trembling body against him and holds me in his strong arms.

"Breathe, Frannie," he softly instructs. Just like he did on the plane. He's going to think I'm some pathetic crazy woman who can't take care of herself. Which is not the case. I'm strong. I'm more than capable of handling my own shit. He just happened to witness me thrown in the middle of two of my biggest fears.

First: heights.

Second: fires.

"Sorry," I mumble.

"Don't be sorry."

"You keep having to save me like I'm some damsel in distress."

He chuckles. "You're not a damsel in distress. I'm sure you could've handled your flight alone and gotten out of the building, too, but I was raised to take care of the women in my life. It's a lesson my grandfather passed down. That's what a man does. He takes care of the people in his life. They step up, care for, and support them, however they can. Right now, Frannie, that's you."

I look up at him and see nothing but sincerity on his face.

"When I was six, the apartment building across from ours caught fire. From my bedroom, Kennedy, Hallie, and I watched the whole thing. Hallie was too little to remember, but it was scary. It wasn't a high rise or anything, but the fire got bad fast and a woman dropped her child out the window into a firefighter's arms, then jumped out herself. One woman was trapped by a falling beam and... she died. Ever since then, I've been terrified of fires. Fire drills at school were hard for me. My parents had to make sure all my teachers knew about my fear of fire so they could check in with me so I wouldn't panic."

"No wonder it scares you. That must have been horrifying to witness. There's nothing wrong with having fears. It's okay to feel exactly how you feel. And luckily, there doesn't seem to be any smoke and I don't see any flames. I'm guessing this was a false alarm."

I breathe out a shaky breath, feeling even more ridiculous now.

When I finally look at the building, I see he's right. There's no smoke. No flames. I let out a weak laugh.

"Well, thank you for being here for me again. I feel silly now."

"Don't." Despite the soft tone of his voice, his eyes are filled with desire.

Slowly, his head lowers toward mine and his lips brush my lips before he slants his mouth over mine for a deeper kiss.

The same warmth I felt tangled in bed with him, floods me again. My stomach tightens and my nipples harden.

"I'm not wearing a bra," I whisper, breaking our kiss as my eyes drift down to his oversized shirt that makes me look like I'm not wearing any shorts, either.

He laughs and kisses my head as a voice comes through the resort PA system telling us that the alarm was sparked by someone smoking on their balcony with the door to the room open. The fire department is almost done sweeping the hotel to double check that everything is safe, and then we'll be able to get back into our rooms.

"What do you think? Early dinner after we get back inside?"

"As long as I can put some actual clothes on, absolutely."

His husky voice sends a chill down my spine as he rumbles, "Only if I can take them off again later."

Yes, please.

CHAPTER EIGHT

Mark

THIS DINNER IS GOING to be the death of me.

Unlike last night when we were playfully exploring and completely enamored with each other, tonight there's nothing but sweltering tension. We're a volcano waiting to erupt.

We would have *gone off* earlier had it not been for that stupid fire alarm. I'm considering bribing the hotel staff to tell me which asshole it was that set the alarm off. I'd like to have a little chat with him, both for interrupting a perfect moment with Frannie and for scaring the hell out of her.

It kills me that she's so afraid to be taken care of, as if it's some horrible thing. There's no weakness in vulnerability, in letting someone take care of you. It's easy to see how strong she is, but I like taking care of her. She's gotten used to being independent, not relying on others, but I'm hoping for the rest of this vacation she'll let me care for her.

Starting tonight.

When the waiter finally comes to take our plates, he asks if we want dessert. My eyes lock with Frannie's and, at the same time, we both say, "No."

Once the bill has been paid, I have Frannie's hand in mine, and I'm leading her to my suite.

We crash through the door, lips and tongues already tangled in a searing kiss.

I fumble with the button of her shorts, and she pulls back, eyes rolling all over me.

Then impatiently, greedily, we strip each other's clothes off like we're in a race to see who can get the other naked first.

And once she is... God. She's gorgeous. Her tousled, long, light brown hair spills over her shoulders, resting just above her perky pink nipples and big round tits.

Grabbing her, I carry her to the bed and lay her down before climbing over the top of her and tasting those perfectly pebbled buds.

"Mark," she groans, hands roaming down my back and then squeezing my ass.

After a few minutes spent with my lips on her chest, I return to her mouth, kissing her deeply as my cock rocks against her inner thigh.

She claws at my butt, then reaches for my cock, stroking it several times before pulling away and looking up at me.

"Do you have protection?" she asks.

I didn't bring condoms with me, but thankfully, the Evermore stocks their rooms well.

Nodding, I hop off the bed and run into the bathroom, opening the cabinet under the sink and pulling out the box. When I get to Frannie, she's looking at me, horrified.

"You brought a box of condoms on vacation?" her voice is frantic. I told her I was planning on spending this week alone, so I know where her mind is.

"No. If you check your bathroom, you'll find the same thing. I've actually never used the condoms here before. I found them when I was snooping around as a kid, and asked my dad about it —he told me they keep things well-stocked for their guests."

"Oh. Okay, then."

"I promise, Frannie, I didn't come here to hook up with random girls. I came here to spend time alone. And then I met you, and I didn't want to spend time without you."

Shit, that sounds like a line.

Thankfully, it doesn't seem to deter her.

She smiles and says, "Well then, what are you waiting for? Get the condom on and get inside me."

My brow furrows. "Why are you trying to rush through this?"

"I'm not. But sex is the point... right?"

I set the condom to the side and position myself over her again. With my lips hovering over her neck, I whisper, "No. Sex isn't something to be rushed. It's about the experience. Teasing, kissing, foreplay. Sex isn't something you do to get off, it's meant to be savored. And I want to savor you. Starting now."

Slowly, I drag my lips down her naked body, then dip my head between her legs, licking up her center and enjoying her heady flavor.

She lets out a gasp, then a moan. "Ooh. Oh my god."

She reaches for my shoulders, but as I swirl my tongue over her swollen clit, her body shudders and she grabs my hair instead.

"Yes. Please. Oh. Fuck, this feels so good."

My cock could hammer nails at this point and her breathy words aren't helping, but I love that she's vocal.

Bringing a hand up, I circle her pussy with one finger, coating it in her wetness before sliding it inside her. She's so wet there's no resistance, and my cock drips in response.

Her hips buck forward as I gently pump that finger in and out of her.

I softly kiss her clit, then suck it between my lips which elicits a loud cry.

"Yes. Oh god. Suck it harder."

Oh, she knows what she likes and isn't afraid to say it.

I shouldn't be surprised.

Inside her, I pull my finger most of the way out, then curl it, hitting her sweet spot. Then, as she asked, I suck her clit harder, occasionally flicking it with my tongue.

"Yes... yes..." Her hips roll in rhythm with my finger as her legs shake and her toes dig into the sheets. "Oh my god. I'm going to... ah..."

She screams as she falls to pieces, covering my hand and filling my mouth with her delicious flavor.

When she's completely done, I slide my finger out, then kiss up her navel, stopping to tease each nipple before ending at her lips.

"How egotistical will it make you if I tell you you're really good at that?"

I smile big, then kiss her hard.

"Not as egotistical as you telling me I've ruined you for every other guy."

She chuckles. "We'll see about that. Now, what about you?"

Reaching down, she wraps her hand around my length and strokes me.

"You're leaking," she whispers, swirling her thumb over my tip. Then she pulls her hand away and licks my pre-cum off her thumb. I almost come on the spot.

"Fuck my mouth," she says urgently.

I'm sorry, did I just have an aneurysm?

"Wha—what?"

"You got to taste me. I want to taste you. Fuck. My. Mouth."

"Okay," I rasp. "But I want to come in your pussy, not your mouth."

"Fine. Now get over here."

So impatient.

Why am I complaining? No girl has *ever* asked me to fuck her mouth before. Not even a jersey chaser.

I position myself farther up her body, then stroke my length, dripping some pre-cum onto her tongue.

Oh god, I'm not going to last long.

Grabbing my hips, she guides me into her mouth and—oh shit. She's so hot and so tight. And Christ, can she take me deep.

Slowly, I thrust into her mouth, and the moans she makes around my cock make my balls tighten.

Shit.

I move a little faster until I'm actually fucking her mouth, and hell, this is the hottest thing a woman has ever done to me.

So hot I'm temporarily blinded by pleasure. There's a dark haze covering my field of vision.

Oh fuck.

I rip my dick from her mouth and sit back on my heels, slowly moving back down her body.

"I can't keep doing that. Your mouth is too fucking tight." I drag my finger down her jaw. "So fucking perfect."

Grabbing the condom, I tear the package open and roll it on, pinching the tip to make sure we're good. I look back at her one last time, and she grabs my ass.

"Now will you get inside me?"

Grabbing her waist, I line myself up, then thrust deep inside her.

"Like that?" I rumble, lowering my lips to her ear.

"Yes..." she hisses. "Just like that."

"You like it hard?"

"You teased me. You savored me. Now fuck me."

Jesus.

Fisting one hand in her hair, I do just that. Pumping into her hard and fast as she cries out my name.

"You need more?" I ask, sliding my hand between our tangled bodies and pressing my thumb into her clit.

"Flick it. Fast." Her heels dig into my butt as she reaches down and squeezes my balls.

My thumb moves furiously over her clit as I drive into her.

"Yes, yes," she chants, moving at the same pace, pressing against me.

Her head drops against the pillow as her walls tighten.

"Let go, baby. Let me feel you come on my cock."

The hand on my balls drops to the bed, and she tightly grabs the sheets, moaning loudly, and I watch as she comes undone, crying out my name. As her pussy pulses around my cock, I pump faster until black spots cloud my vision and I can't breathe as I explode inside her.

So good. So fucking good.

My body heaves as I collapse on the bed next to her, wrapping my arms around her and pulling her close.

"That was..." she trails off. "Oh god... amazing."

"God's not here, baby. Just me."

She smacks my chest but laughs, then finds my lips with hers. "That was seriously incredible. I might be addicted now."

At that, an evil grin appears on my face. "I hope you were planning to spend most of this vacation in bed, then."

"I'm open to discussing it."

"So, what you're saying is, I was right about savoring it."

"I can admit when I'm wrong. And you were right. So deliciously fucking right."

"Good answer."

She yawns as I kiss her cheek.

Before we both fall asleep, we clean up, then end up back in bed, wrapped in each other's arms again.

The last thought I have as we drift off is... *I'm so screwed. I'm actually falling for this girl.*

CHAPTER NINE
TUESDAY

Mark

FOR THE FIRST time in a very long time, I struggle to peel my eyes open. Bright sunlight burns my retinas the second I open my eyes, and I tightly shut them again.

Trying again, I shield my eyes from the sun, then slowly open them. My first glance is at the clock. No way. It's after nine? God, I can't remember the last time I slept that late.

Of course, I also don't remember the last time I stayed up half the night having sex.

Despite falling asleep after our first round, since it was only eight at night, we both woke up an hour later and got right down to business again. And one more time. It was almost one in the morning before we passed out for good.

My eyes move down to the bed where Frannie is curled up against me, her head nestled against my pec. She's gorgeous. Hair splayed over the pillows, bathed in sunlight, her curves and soft skin on full display. One toned leg is tossed over mine, and her hand is on my stomach.

My dick is thrilled to have her in such close proximity and is reaching out, begging for more play time.

Easy, tiger. Let's wait till she wakes up.

Carefully, I reach behind me and grab my phone off the bedside table. I have several texts. A group text from Hardy and Ackley, and one from Coach Robbins.

I check the one from Coach first.

COACH ROBBINS

Looks like official reports will be filed later this week. Keep flying under the radar, son.

I let out a slow breath and reply.

Good. I'll still be on vacation, so hopefully I won't have to worry too much about the press. Glad he'll finally get what he deserves.

COACH ROBBINS

Let's hope so.

When I look back at Frannie, guilt courses through me. When I lied to her on the plane, I felt bad, but I had no idea we'd end up tangled in bed together after by far the best sex of my life. I know I need to tell her the truth, but damn, it's nice not to think about that part of my life.

Not wanting to get into a ridiculous conversation with Ackley and Hardy right now, I put my phone back on the bedside table without checking our group text.

"Mm... what are you doing?" Frannie mumbles against my chest.

I sweep some hair off her face. "Nothing. Go back to sleep."

Her eyes flash open. "Why? You seem nice and awake." Then her hand is on my cock and it's game over.

Rolling over, I pin her against the bed and kiss her hungrily.

Screw eating, screw working out, screw anything else. All I want is to live in this bed with her all day. And by how quickly she grabs a condom and rips it open, it seems she wants the same.

AFTER A LONG MORNING spent in bed, then the shower, and the bathroom counter—I think I've broken my record for number of times having sex in a twenty-four-hour period—Frannie and I finally left the hotel room and rented some bikes. We biked the few blocks into town and enjoyed brunch at the diner, then went to the bookstore, which features lots of authors local to this area of South Carolina. After searching for a bit, we found a fantasy series that interested us both, and bought the two copies of the first book that the store had in stock. Frannie was excited because apparently she knows one of the male narrators—Justin Ayers—who is a friend of her cousin Kennedy.

After that, we explored more of the town before coming back here for a late afternoon spent on the beach and in the outdoor pool with a swim-up bar. Now we're enjoying dinner on the patio. After all the sex last night and today, there's significantly less tension between us, and we've enjoyed our meals more.

I also told Frannie it was okay to get a second drink, and I'd cut her off after that. I got a call from my coach a few minutes ago, and stepped away from the table to take it, though I made sure to tell our server not to bring Frannie any more drinks before I did.

Coach didn't have much new to report, other than the investigator being almost finished and his report will be up soon, and Jeff's soon to be ex-wife hired a shark of a lawyer and has offered to pay for an equally good lawyer for the woman Jeff assaulted. Apparently, she's ready to take the bastard down.

Now I'm standing in front of the bathroom mirror giving myself a pep talk. Two drinks in, and Frannie shouldn't be drunk, which means I can tell her now about my career and real name and what's going on. Maybe I'll get lucky and she'll be relaxed enough that she won't be mad. I glance down at my watch and realize how long I've been gone.

Shit.

I turn and hurry out of the men's room, then make my way back to our table.

When I sit down, I find a very relaxed Frannie sipping on a drink. Or guzzling. Which gives me pause, because when I left, her glass was nearly empty. That's when I realize there's another glass on the table. When she got her second, they took her first glass away, which means she's on her third.

I should not have left her alone. I promised her I wouldn't let her drink too much. And where the hell is our server? I specifically told him not to... I look around and realize another server is working our section now. The other guy must've gone on break.

"Frannie, slow down," I say, putting my hand over hers.

She looks up at me and squints one eye. "It's fineeee." She draws out the word and I cringe. "It's only my second refill." She narrows both eyes and looks up. "Second refill of my second drink. That's..." she counts on her fingers. "Four. Right?"

I swallow hard. "Right."

She claps her hands together, then throws them up in the air. "See? I can still count. I'm good. Good. All good."

As she drops her hands, she loses her balance and nearly falls out of her chair. I lunge across the table to steady her.

"Babe, I think it's time to head back to your room."

She pouts. "No. I'm having fun. And these drinks are"—she hiccups—"good."

Christ, what have I done?

"I'm sure they are. They're also full of tequila." *To kill ya,* as Grandpa likes to say.

She sighs. "Okay. I guess." She hiccups again. Then burps and grimaces. "Yeah, maybe my room," she slurs.

I flag down the waiter, pay for our meal and the half bottle of tequila Frannie has likely imbibed, then take her hand, pulling her up from the table. She careens backward, so I steady her, then lift her into my arms.

"What are you doin'?" she slurs.

"Carrying your drunk butt back to the room."

"I'm not... drunk."

"You're right. You blew through tipsy and drunk to wasted, babe. Let's get you back to your room."

"Well... okay. As long as you promise to stay and do that thing with your tongue on my—"

"Babe, I will do whatever you want, but for now, let's shh," I say, carrying her through the lobby—which is full of people side-eyeing us.

"Okerr," she mumbles against my chest.

It's going to be a long night.

FRANNIE RETCHES and leans over the toilet, puking for the third time in twenty minutes. The good news is, it should all be out of her soon. I already had the desk send up several flavors of Gatorade and a few types of crackers for when she gets through this. Immediate rehydration and something gentle to settle the stomach are key to avoiding a horrendous hangover. It might be too late for her, though.

I rub her back as she sits back on her butt. She's wearing those tiny sleep shorts again, and her ass keeps sticking to the floor. She's also wearing a soft tank-top style bralette, and I tucked her hair back as soon as we got back to her room.

"I'm sorry," she cries, wiping her mouth.

"Don't be. I promised I wouldn't let you drink too much."

"I should be capable of being responsible. Why am I like this? How do I lose track of how many drinks I've had? What does alcohol do to me? Oh my god! Am I an alcoholic? I have one and I can't say no to more?"

"No. The alcohol disorients you and lowers your inhibitions. I'm sorry I left you alone."

"It's not your fault." She gags again and dives forward, but only throws up a little bit. "I think I'm done," she mutters.

I reach up and flush the toilet, then help her up. Her legs are shaking, so I carry her back to bed and tuck her in, then bring her some Gatorade.

After a few sips, she lets out a breath. "This is not how I wanted our night to go. If you want to leave, you can. You can avoid me for the rest of the trip—"

"Why would I want to do that?"

"Because I'm a hot mess. You've seen me get stupid drunk, practically cry on the flight down here, and nearly go catatonic over a fire alarm. You should be running for the hills right now."

Maybe she's right. Maybe I should. But that's the last thing I want. I like taking care of her. I like that she's let her guard down enough to let me comfort her.

That sets off an unsettling feeling in my gut. What the hell are we doing? I haven't told her the truth about who I am. We met on a plane. We're on vacation. By nature, this whole thing has an expiration date. But I can't shake the feeling that I don't want it to. That, in turn, sends me spiraling about what that means, what we're doing, and if I want more with her.

Nope. Too much for right now. Let's just enjoy where we are.

"I'm sorry," she mutters again.

"Stop apologizing. You're not perfect, and I wasn't expecting perfection. You knew your body well enough to know you shouldn't order another drink, but I encouraged you to and took responsibility, then I didn't follow through. I'm sorry about that. But I think we should both stop apologizing. I'm going to find something to watch, then you're going to eat some crackers."

She grimaces and whimpers.

"Once you get past the first few bites, you'll feel better, I promise."

"Okay. But I want to watch *Shadow and Bone.* I'm obsessed with that show. Have you seen it?"

"Can't say that I have." I stand up and grab the remote and some crackers.

"You might like it. Either way, it's my comfort show, so you're stuck with it... if you're staying." Her voice is hushed and her eyes are filled with vulnerability.

I look back at her again, wanting her to feel sure of my words. "I'm staying. I'll be here all night."

"Okay, then."

She takes the remote and finds the show, then grabs a pack of crackers and nibbles on one.

I flick off the lamp and get comfortable in bed next to her.

As the theme song plays, Frannie looks up at me, cracker in hand, and whispers, "Thank you for taking care of me."

My heart beats erratically, and again that uncertain feeling gnaws at my gut. *What are we doing?*

CHAPTER TEN
THURSDAY

Frannie

I AM AN IDIOT.

For many reasons, but right now, because I made the mistake of telling Hallie and Kennedy I slept with Mark, and they've gone off the deep end. If they aren't sending me wedding dress pictures, they're trying to convince me to let them video chat with him, or they want me to give them his full name and birth date so they can run a background check and/or cyber stalk him.

They crossed the line from funny to crazy a while ago, and I'm tired of their shenanigans.

Especially because they're taking this to a serious place, and... let's face it, Mark and I have an expiration date. I'm only here for a total of ten days. He's here for fourteen. That means in five more days, I'll leave and he'll still be here. Who knows if we'll see each other again? We haven't talked about any of that, and I'm trying not to think about it and just enjoy where we are. And how unbelievably sweet he is.

It's not easy for me to let my guard down, but each day he proves more and more worthy of seeing the vulnerable sides of me. Of course, some of them he's gotten whether I wanted to show them or not.

Case in point: me getting horrendously drunk and puking for twenty minutes straight the other night. The way he took care of me... *swoon.*

In the moment, I felt awful about the situation but appreciated how sweet he was. After the fact? Yeah, his attentiveness and caring had me all hot and bothered. And once I was feeling well enough yesterday, I dropped to my knees and thanked him with my mouth.

Luckily for me, yesterday was a rainy day, so we stayed in, which gave me time to recover from the previous night's stupidity. This is why I have the one drink rule. But despite that, yesterday was a lot of fun. We alternated between watching *Shadow and Bone*—which Mark is now obsessed with as well—and reading the fantasy books we bought at the local bookstore. Oh, and eventually, having sex too. Because speaking of me being an idiot... I've been dumb as hell about sex.

I'm not sure if I always rushed through sex because I thought I was supposed to, or the guys weren't fulfilling me the way I needed them to—even though I've always been fairly vocal in bed and usually get off. I've never gotten off like I do with Mark, though. Multiple O's, the sinfully delicious feeling of our sweaty bodies tangled up under the sheets, the extra boldness I feel with him. He makes me want to be naughty. Jesus Christ, if he ever calls me *good girl,* I'll probably come on the spot.

God, now I want to hear him say that.

I need to get my mind out of the gutter, though, because right now, we're doing the thing I was most excited about when I booked this trip... a dolphin tour.

Since I was a little kid, I've been obsessed with dolphins. At this moment, I'm wearing an anklet with sterling silver dolphins on it. I've always found them beautiful, fascinating creatures. Not to mention my obsession with *Flipper* as a kid, too.

We're on the back of a boat for a private dolphin tour. They take us to popular dolphin hangouts and, hopefully, we get to watch some dolphins playing and having fun. I'm trying not to get my hopes up too much, but I'm excited.

I was planning to do one of the group tours, but Mark surprised me with this private one. He must make bank doing finance or whatever he does with numbers, because he's insisted on paying for everything. The most he let me buy was coffee when we were out biking the other day.

"Whoa," Mark says, at the same time the guide says, "Looks like you'll be getting quite a show."

The skipper kills the engines and we watch as dolphins flip and twist through the air only a hundred feet or so away from us.

I watch two of them nuzzle together and squawk at each other, while two more leap and chase each other around in the waves. Another does jump and flip after jump and flip.

My hand is intertwined with Mark's as I watch them raptly, the kid in me overjoyed to see them this close.

We watch them play happily for a while. I don't care about the hot as hell midday sun or anything else. I'm in love.

The boat rocks suddenly, and then again. Mark and I look at the tour guide, who points to the end of the boat.

Oh my god.

A dolphin pops up from under the water, and then another.

I gasp and squeal, seeing them mere feet from me.

Mindlessly, I start talking to them.

"What are you two doing? Are you having fun?"

They squawk back at me, then dive under the water again before popping back up and blowing water out. They make a noise like they're laughing, then one jumps and twists.

It's only when Mark wraps an arm around me, I realize I'm crying.

"Frannie?"

"Sorry. I'm fine. Just another little quirk about me. I love dolphins, and I've dreamed of seeing them up close and personal in the wild like this since I was a little kid. It's a literal dream come true. I'm sure that sounds dumb."

"It's not dumb. This is really fucking cool. I had no idea how much you love dolphins, but I know I've enjoyed this every time I've done it. The private tours are even better than the group ones because it's just us and the dolphins."

I lean against him. "Thank you," I whisper. "This is one of the coolest things anyone has ever done for me. I'll never forget this."

"Good." He sweeps his hand up the side of my face then drops his head and captures my lips in a passionate kiss. Overcome with emotion, I wrap my hand around his neck and pull him closer, parting my lips as we deepen the kiss, tongues dancing. This kiss is as magical as the experience we're living right now. I'm still amazed I get to have either.

When I planned this vacation, I had no idea it would end up being one of the most memorable times of my life. It's only halfway over, but I already know I'll never forget a moment of this.

There's a splash, then another spray of water. We pull apart, laughing as the dolphins squawk back at us.

Mark squeezes my hand, and I rest my head on his shoulder, watching the dolphins play more as my stomach twists with a mixture of warmth and fear. I'm falling hard for him, but I have no idea if he feels the same or if he'll want to see me again after this week. With that bittersweet thought in my head, I focus on our dolphin friends, determined to enjoy every second of this—and my time with Mark—since I don't know if I'll ever experience either again.

CHAPTER ELEVEN
SATURDAY

MY HEART POUNDS and my lungs burn, but I push myself harder. Three days without working out—besides bedroom cardio, which I fully admit is much more fun—and I've been itching for a run. Since I'm tired of lathering up my entire chest and back to run outside, I chose a treadmill in the hotel's gym.

My phone screen lights up with a call from my cousin, Rae. Swiping to answer, I quickly put it on speaker.

"Hey, kid."

"Kid? Really? You're like three years older."

"Exactly, *kid.*"

"Ugh. Why did I call you?" she sasses. The Abbott women are known to be strong, fierce, and sassy as fuck. My sister was outnumbered three to one growing up, and you'd never have known it. She can put us all in our place without so much as a glance in our direction.

"Got me."

"Rude. I called because Aaron and I will be in Ida this weekend for February break. Sarah and Joel, too. And since Dani is in Ida now as well, we thought we could have a family night if you can spare a couple of days to come visit us."

"I'd love that, but I'll have to take a rain check. I'm on vacation."

"You take vacations?"

"You're spicy today. Did you get laid this morning or something? Not that I actually want to know." She cackles, giving me the answer I didn't need and causing me to gag. "You know damn well where I take vacations—besides Ida or back home."

"Anais Bay?" she asks in surprise. "No way. I—"

In the background, I hear her husband, Aaron, say, "Hey, Beautiful, we have to go."

"Shoot, sorry. I've got to run. Study group time. Let me know when you'll be in Ida next! Love you."

"Love you too. Bye."

She hangs up, and I click my phone screen off again, then turn the treadmill up, running faster.

The thought of visiting Ida now sends a wave of uncertainty through me. I've enjoyed every second of this vacation that I've spent with Frannie, but what comes next? Do I really believe this is some written in the stars shit? That we're *meant to be?* Should I keep seeing her in Ida? I could. Easily. But it wouldn't be easy once the season starts up again. How would she even deal with all that? Especially since she doesn't even know the truth.

Yep, I'm still an asshole on that front.

When I'm with her, she's all I'm thinking about, so I've got to make a decision on this when I'm *not* with her.

Or maybe...

If I can't stop thinking about her when I'm with her, maybe that means I should continue things. That I'll miss her when we're apart.

That sounds like a load of bullshit. Tomorrow it'll be a week since I met her. Only a week. It's insane that I feel this way. I'm probably high on vacation life.

My phone goes off again, this time with a video call from Hardy. Welcoming the distraction, I answer.

"Ooh, there's our boy. Looking hot, Markie," Hardy says as he and Ackley appear on the screen. They're sitting at Hardy's kitchen counter.

"Shut up. You know I don't like running with a shirt on."

"Oh, we know. The fabric sticks to you, it makes you sweatier, you get too hot, then you feel gross," Ackley spouts, listing the points I often make when someone asks why I don't put a shirt on when I run.

While I can run outside in any temperature, I prefer not to unless I can go shirtless. Otherwise, it's on the treadmill at home.

"Exactly."

"So, what's good down there? You having fun with your holiday honey?" Hardy asks.

"Holiday honey?"

"You know, holiday, like vacation?" Ackley supplies.

"Uh, sure. It's good."

"Just good? My man, you haven't sent a text that was more than four words in the same number of days. I don't think it's because you're thrilled with the ocean views. It's because you're balls deep in—"

"Okay. That's enough. Yes, I'm having fun with Frannie. No, it's not some *Girls Gone Wild* spring break hookup. We're enjoying each other's company."

Hardy smacks Ackley in the chest. "Oh, did you hear that? They're having a lovely time enjoying each other's company." He puts on a British accent to mock me. It's terrible, but you have to admire his commitment. "Does the governess allow you two to sit on the same sofa? Must you leave six inches of space between you? Only touch during approved dances?"

Ackley snickers in the background.

"Where are you getting this shit?" I ask.

"He's been watching *Bridgerton,*" Ackley explains.

"Seriously?"

"Don't knock it till you try it. That drama is fire."

"Whatever you say."

I turn the treadmill down, ready for a short cooldown.

"Did you call for any other reason than to mock me?"

"Nah. We just wanted to see how you were. Coach said the news will go out on Tuesday. How you feelin' about that?"

I shrug one shoulder. "Is what it is. I don't want to be dealing with it, but it's better than having the people he hurt have to deal with it. I know they will, but I'll take the heat as long as I can."

"You've got a hero complex," Ackley says.

"No, I don't." I don't think. Do I? I just like doing what I can to help others. I don't need to be the hero. Hell, right now, in the world's eyes, I'm a villain. And besides the tabloids' endless interest in me, it doesn't bother me at all. "You guys are in the same boat as me. I just happened to punch the fucker and get the media's attention."

"Yeah. You're also the QB. People love a QB," Hardy says.

"Well, I'm trying not to think about all that shit here. It'll be waiting when I get back."

"And what about your holiday honey?"

I roll my eyes, but say, "I don't know. We'll see."

Ackley throws a twenty on the counter. "Twenty bucks says they come back engaged."

Hardy fishes out his wallet and chucks a twenty down as well. "I say they'll be married."

"And I say you're both crazy. Have a good day. Bye."

I hang up as they're saying goodbye, then turn the treadmill down slower for another minute before turning it off completely and heading back up to my room.

I'M SUPPOSED to meet Frannie in twenty minutes for a late lunch. I took a long shower, but haven't figured out what I want to do with her. Maybe I should ease off spending time with her now, so we're not as attached when this all ends.

Except I don't want to do that.

I know when it's time to call in an expert. Or maybe two.

Grabbing my phone, I dial my grandfather's number. He answers on the first ring.

"Well, if it isn't the prodigal football player. How are you doing? Enjoying Anais Bay?"

"Hey, Gramps. I'm all right. How about you?"

"How many times have I told you I hate it when you call me Gramps?"

"Why do you think I do it?" I ask, sitting down on the edge of the bed.

Gram's laughter fills my ear. "Grandpa has his girlies, and I have my troublemaking boys. You sound just like him when he was your age. Or any age."

"Oh, shush," Grandpa says, but Gram laughs again. "Is there a reason for this call? Or did you two just want to gang up and heckle me?"

Letting out a sigh, I rub the back of my neck. "There's a reason. But I need honest answers from both of you. Not the party line."

"And what's the party line?" Gram asks.

"That love will solve all your problems and it's the best thing in the world and it happens in an instant and—"

"Sonny, I think you've missed the point of what we've been saying all these years if you think *that* is the party line. So, speaking of no bullshit, how about you tell us what's going on?"

"You know everything that happened with the team. I needed a break, so I'm down in Anais Bay. On the flight down, I met this incredible woman. The second I sat down next to her, I was drawn to her."

"Why?" Grandpa asks. "Because she looks nice?"

"No. I think she's gorgeous, but that's not why I was drawn to her. She was hunched over and panicking about the flight. I offered her my hand if she got scared, and when she grabbed it I..."

"You what?" Gram prods.

"I felt something. Like electricity or some... shit."

There's silence for a moment and I realize it's because they're trying not to laugh.

"You hear that, Ma? Mark *felt* something." Grandpa says, finally giving in to his laughter. My grandparents have called each other Ma and Pa forever. They got used to saying it after they had my dad—who is the oldest in his family—and started calling each other that all the time. Unless Gram is annoyed, then she uses his full name.

"You don't have to pick on me, old man."

"Oh, we're not picking, honey. But all these years, you've seemed to think love was a myth despite how much of it surrounds you," Gram says.

"I didn't say I was in love with her," I protest. Because I'm not. Feelings? Yes. Love. No. Not yet.

"Well, how do you think love starts? That connection you feel is the seed. The more time you spend cultivating it, the deeper it grows. And when it takes root, those roots are love. The question isn't whether you felt something, it's whether you have the balls to acknowledge that and let it grow."

Well, I wanted real talk.

Grandpa never disappoints.

"Sweetheart, love doesn't happen in a day. Yes, people talk about love at first sight, but despite what even your grandfather might say, that's not how it works. It takes time to love someone, to know them. But that connection, the spark that ignites and draws you to another person, that can happen in an instant. You can fight it or accept it, but if it's meant to lead to love, there's no stopping it. Only foolish people try to avoid or deny it and end up hurting themselves and the other person along the way. If you like this girl and want to spend more time with her, then you should. Your schedule may make it harder sometimes, but during the off-season, you could be anywhere. Don't hold yourself back because you're afraid."

Gram never disappoints, either.

Huffing out a sigh, I mumble, "She lives in Ida."

"Well, sonny, that sounds like fate. And you know what I say about fate..."

"I do."

"You have to decide what you want, but by the fact that you're calling us, I think you already know," Gram says gently.

She's right. They're both right. They're both *always* right. How do they do that?

"There's one more problem."

"What's that?" Grandpa asks, unamused now.

"She doesn't know who I really am. I lied on the plane because I didn't know we'd end up seeing each other beyond the flight. She thinks I'm Mark Hainley, numbers guy. Not Mark Abbott, professional football player."

"It's understandable why you wouldn't share that information initially. Tell her now," Grandpa says.

"I know I need to. I'm worried she's going to be mad..."

"Mark." Gram's voice has an edge to it. "How long have you been lying to her?"

"Just a week but..."

"You've been with her?" Gram asks.

"Yes," I admit, hanging my head as if they can see me.

"How many times did I tell you boys, you never lie to get into bed with a woman?" Grandpa asks, his voice commanding.

"I didn't lie so she'd sleep with me. I lied. The rest happened later."

"Tell her," Grandpa says firmly. "You owe her the truth. Not only who you are, but what you want. She deserves to know it all."

"Yeah. Thanks," I say quietly.

"You'll sort it all out," Gram says reassuringly.

I'd better. Because I want to see her again. I don't know why I've been hiding from this. From the moment I met her, Frannie pulled me in and all I've wanted is more.

"Thank you both. I should go. Love you."

"Love you too, sweetheart. Bye."

The call ends, and I set my phone to the side.

I'm not used to opening myself up, being vulnerable. Maybe when I was young, but through college and playing in the league, I learned to keep it under lock and key. Letting someone new in wasn't worth the risk. But Frannie is worth it. This instant connection thing is still new to me, but Gram is right, I'd be a fool if I tried to deny it. And I don't think I want to.

AFTER A LAZY AFTERNOON spent walking on the beach while Frannie looked for seashells, we enjoyed dinner on the patio. The weather has been phenomenal this entire trip. Normally, the daytime temperatures are in the low seventies this time of year, but they've been around eighty all week, and it only rained one day.

Frannie and I are on the beach again, this time looking at the stars over the ocean. The sky has a greenish-blue hue that is absolutely stunning.

"This is beautiful. A perfect night," Frannie says softly, but there's a wistfulness in her voice.

"Are you okay?" I ask, looking down at her.

She nods slowly, then looks back at the ocean. "I've had a great time with you."

"There's a but coming, isn't there?"

She bites her lip as she looks up at me.

"I think we should spend the rest of our vacation separately. I love spending time with you, but knowing that it's all going to end in a few days... I can't let myself get more attached. I've spent a lot of time thinking today, and I know myself well enough to know it'll crush me to say goodbye to you if we keep this going any longer."

My stomach lurches, and my heart pounds as everything inside me screams *no!*

My grandparents were right. I've known what I want this whole time. I've just been too chicken to admit it.

Cupping her cheek, I look into her gorgeous blue eyes, which have turned a similar color as the sky.

"I don't want to stop."

"I know. I don't either, but Mark—"

"No. I mean when vacation is over. I don't want to stop seeing you. I've been planning to spend some time in Ida. I want to spend it with you."

Her eyes light. "You mean that? Please don't say it if you don't."

I graze my lips over hers. "I mean it. I want you. I want this. And I want to see where it goes back in the real world."

She throws her arms around my neck and kisses me. Relief floods my body. It still feels a little crazy, but I don't want to lose this girl. I want more.

Threading her hair, I hold her head in place as I deepen our kiss.

I want so much more.

Frannie

ON THE LIST of crazy decisions I've made in my life, falling for the guy I met on a plane is probably near the top. Above the time I decided blunt bangs were a good idea. Below the time I decided to move to Ida on a whim. One of those worked out well. The other? Well, let's just say some photos needed to be burned.

This decision? I guess we'll see how it plays out.

Not that falling for him has been much of a decision at all. Especially with his mouth crushing against mine and his tongue delving deep and wrestling with mine.

Falling for him wasn't a choice, but trusting him is. Trust isn't an easy thing for me to hand over, but so far, he's proven himself to be sweet, thoughtful, and gentlemanly.

Except for right now when he's stripping me down and tossing me onto the bed. Climbing over the top of me and kissing me deeply as I fumble with the button of his shorts.

There's definitely nothing gentlemanly about the way he slides his finger inside me and swirls his thumb over my clit while whispering all the dirty things he's going to do to me.

Once he's naked, he wraps his arms around my back, then rolls over, flipping us so I'm on top. He grabs my hips and huskily says, "Come here."

"What?"

I'm already sitting on him.

He licks his lower lip.

"Come here and sit on my face."

Oh god.

"Are—are you sure? Will you even be able to breathe?"

His grip on my hips tightens. "I'll be fine. Get over here and let me eat your pussy."

"Okay," I squeak, scooting up his body.

"Closer." I shimmy so I'm centered over his mouth. "Lower," he rumbles.

Still worried I'm going to suffocate him, I drop my hips.

"Good girl."

Shit.

"That was sexy as fuck, but please don't say it again unless you want me to come before you even touch me."

He arches a brow and smirks before grabbing my thighs and holding me in place. Then his lips are on my clit, and I can't breathe. Can't see. Can't think.

I grab the headboard as he licks me in long, lavish strokes. My hips roll in rhythm with his tongue. He uses the tip of his tongue to flick my clit and I nearly black out.

What the fuck is happening?

Shamelessly, I ride his face.

"Oh, Mark..."

My stomach clenches and I know I won't last much longer.

I move my hips faster as he slides one finger inside me.

"Yes..." I whimper.

"Come for me, baby."

I'm so close.

My walls tighten around his finger. I'm seconds away. And then he says...

"Come on my face like a good girl."

I explode like fireworks. Loud, colorful fireworks.

Overstimulated, I lift my hips, but my legs are shaking so hard I almost collapse.

Mark steadies my thighs as I catch my breath.

"Holy fuck, that was intense."

"Hot as hell. Gorgeous. Watching you come... goddamn, Frannie. I've never seen anything sexier."

I lift an eyebrow and smile as I slide down his body. "Really?" I ask, lifting my hips. "Not even me riding your cock?"

I sink down on him, letting him feel my wet heat bare.

"Frannie," he groans. "Condom. Now. I won't last much longer."

Lifting my hips again, I grab a condom, tear open the package, and slowly slide it on before gliding down his length again.

He groans at the contact, and it's now my mission to make him feel as good as he made me feel.

Swirling my hips, I slowly move up and down his shaft, playing with my nipples, more for his benefit than mine, because my body is still riding the crazy high he just gave me.

Moaning whenever he hits the deepest part of me, I swirl my hips faster.

His hands slide up to my waist, and he holds me in place as he drives up into me.

Fuck, that feels good.

I fall into rhythm with him, rotating my hips faster and faster until his fingers dig into my skin and his eyes close halfway.

Leaning forward, I run my hands up his chest, riding him even harder.

"Come. Right now. Fill my pussy."

"Fuck, Frannie," he groans, then goes off like a rocket, his body shaking and his eyes rolling back.

Now *that* is the sexiest thing ever.

Lifting myself off him, I lie down on the bed next to him, resting my hand on his chest. His heart is still pounding.

He leans over and kisses my forehead.

"You're amazing."

I kiss his stubbled jaw.

"You're not so bad yourself."

After cleaning up, we end up back in bed, tangled in each other's arms.

This is not how I thought tonight would go.

The other day, after we watched the dolphins, all I wanted to do was cry. Partly because I was sad such a phenomenal experience was over, and partly because I knew if I was that sad over the dolphins, I would be a mess over Mark. I tried to shake it off, but I couldn't, and when he said he wanted to work out this morning, I was happy to let him go. While he was gone, I thought it all through, and I knew I had to end things. Every day we've grown closer, and I wouldn't have been able to handle the hurt if I didn't stop myself.

When I told him we needed to stop this, I wasn't expecting him to say he wanted more. A sliver of me hoped for it, but I didn't want to believe it. I'm still a little surprised, to be honest.

"Still want more of this?" I whisper. I say it playfully, but the truth is, I need to hear him say it again.

"After tonight? Hell yes."

"So you want more sex?" There's more sharpness to my voice than I wanted, but I can't help it. If that's all he wants, this was a mistake. A hot, sinful mistake.

His eyes flash open and he brushes his hand over my cheek. "Of course, I want more of that. But I also want more of this. You in my arms. I want more of us, Frannie. Whether it's low-key dinners or crazy moments, or quiet afternoons—I want more. And I want to know what we can be."

I relax at those words.

"I want that too."

"Good. Come here."

He pulls me closer, and I nestle in against him.

Though a part of me is still skeptical—it all seems too easy—here, in his arms, it's hard to notice anything else but how peaceful I feel.

CHAPTER THIRTEEN
SUNDAY

Frannie

EVERY DAY this trip gets better and better—except for the dolphins. Nothing will top that. Mark is out for a run now, and I'm lying on my bed messing with my phone and reliving the trip thus far, especially today.

This morning, Mark and I went snorkeling. I wasn't sure I'd be any good at it, but it ended up being really fun. We got to see so many cool fish and sea creatures. I'm definitely going again before this trip is over. *We* are. I'm still wrapping my head around what Mark said last night. He wants us to keep seeing each other once this trip is over. He's even considering changing his flight to fly back with me. However, since I took a full two weeks off, I'm considering changing my flight and staying longer. I'm sure Mark wouldn't mind me rooming with him for a few days, given that we've spent every night in the same room since we first slept together.

I'm trying not to get my hopes up too high. There's still that nagging feeling in the back of my mind that if it seems too good to be true, it probably is. But at the same time, I've seen plenty of my friends find their true loves and get their happily ever afters. Hell, one of my friends just married the love of her life a few months ago, a boy she met when she was five and had an epic best friends-to-lovers romance with. I missed the wedding because I'd already made plans to visit my biological father, and since we're still building our relationship, that took precedence for me. Between her and some of the other friends I've made in Ida, it's hard not to believe that kind of love exists. I have no idea if that's the path Mark and I are headed down, but I don't believe it's impossible anymore, either.

I smile when a text pops up from that same friend, who is also the one who referred me here.

I was uncertain at best at the start of this trip, but I'm in love with Anais Bay now, and it's been one of my best vacations ever.

RAE

Hey! How's the vacation going?

> Me: Great! I seriously can't thank you enough
> for referring me here. It's been incredible!

RAE

I'm so glad. My best friend has a beach house
in Charleston, so that's where we usually go,
but the few times I've been to Anais Bay, it's
been beautiful.

RAE

Oh! By the way, let me know if you run into
any football players.

> What?

RAE

My cousin is on vacation there right now too! I
had no idea he was going to be there,
otherwise, I'd have given you his number.

There's an uncertain prick in my stomach. Rae's cousin.

> I'll be on the lookout. What's his name?

Please, please don't say...

RAE

> Mark Abbott. Though when he travels, he sometimes goes by

I flick my phone screen off. I don't need to read the rest of the text to know what it says. *Hainley.*

My hands shake and tears spring to my eyes. *There's the other shoe dropping. The moment where I clearly see it* is *too good to be true. And it always has been.* Because he's been lying to me. Since the moment I met him, he's been lying to me. And maybe that was one thing on the plane. But we've slept together. He told me he wanted to continue this in Ida. He could've told me the truth many times. He *should* have. But he didn't.

Turning the screen on again, I ignore the texts from Rae and flip to my browser. I open it and search his name. *Mark Abbott.*

Loads of articles and photos come up. Fistfights. Jealousy. Ruining his career.

I don't click on any of it. I don't need to know what people who don't know him are saying about him. Instead, I flip to the images on the tiniest chance that I'm wrong, but as soon as I see the first one, I know I'm not. That curly auburn hair is unmistakable.

Fuck.

I fell for it. I fell for everything he said. I... I'm such an idiot.

And perfectly timed, as soon as I turn my phone screen off, the door to my room swings open and *he* walks in. Smiling like the lying jackass he is.

"Hey, baby." He strides over and kisses my cheek. It takes everything inside me not to slap him.

"Hi. Good run?" I ask, struggling to keep my voice even.

"Yeah. What have you been up to?" he asks, walking toward the bathroom.

"Oh, I was just texting my friend. You know, the one who recommended this place. I'm not sure I mentioned her name before." At the tone of my voice, he spins around.

"Uh, no. I don't think you did."

"It's Rae." His eyes widen, and he opens his mouth, but I don't stop. "Rae Cooper. Formerly McKinley. But you already know that. Don't you, Mark *Abbott?*"

The color drains from his face.

"Frannie. I—" he chokes out, but I hold my hand up.

"Don't. I don't need to hear anything else from you." I climb off the bed and walk over to the dresser, grabbing my key card and shoving it into my pocket. "This was my fault. I let myself believe that this fling was something more. That I was more than an easy hookup on your vacation." I shove my feet into my shoes and turn toward the door.

"Frannie, stop. I didn't lie about my feelings for you—what I want—"

"Stop. You've told me the last lie you're going to tell me. I'm going for a walk. When I get back, I want you gone."

"Frannie—"

"Goodbye, Mark."

Despite my shaking hands, I walk out of the room with my head held high. No matter how I'm feeling on the inside, I refuse to let him see me break.

BLOOD SURGES through my veins as my cheeks heat and sweat pours out of me.

The midday sun is gruesome, but it's not hotter than the

anger burning in my gut. Anger at him for lying to me. Anger at myself for believing it.

This is why I'm running. In tiny pajama shorts, a baggy tank, and sneakers that were not made for running. My socks sit lower than the heel of my shoe and painful blisters are already forming.

Luckily, I've barely noticed because I'm in the middle of a heated internal debate. Call this trip a loss and go home early. Go back to the resort and avoid Mark for the rest of the trip. *Or,* a little voice inside me nags, *hear him out.*

But he lied.

About something small.

If he could lie about that tiny thing with ease, there's no telling what else he could lie about. Just one lie could destroy everything. I mean, what if he's serious about wanting to continue things with me. Say I gave in. We moved past this, started dating, maybe even got married. Then he's in a different city with girls throwing themselves at him. All it would take is one little lie.

Is that worth it? Worth my heart and my pain?

"Frannie!" a voice calls from behind me.

No.

I pick up my speed.

"Frannie." The voice is closer now.

I keep going, hauling ass up the center street in town as my heels undoubtedly bleed against the back of my shoes.

"Are you really going to make me chase you?" Mark says, a few steps behind me now.

Screw it.

I stop abruptly and turn to face him. Stupid quarterback who runs every morning and is in perfect shape. I'd never be able to outrun him, no matter how hard I tried.

He jerks to a stop in front of me, nearly tumbling into me.

"Sorry. I wasn't expecting you to stop."

"What, were you going to chase me all the way back to the resort?"

"Well, eventually, I would've just run beside you."

"What do you want, Mark?" I snap.

"To apologize. When I got on the plane to come here, it was the first time I'd felt any relief in weeks. I'm all over the tabloids right now and not for good reasons. Not for true reasons. I understand your hatred of lies, Frannie, because I've been a victim of plenty. I should've told you the truth the morning after our date, once I knew I wanted to spend every second of this vacation with you, but I didn't. There's no good reason for that, other than me being afraid."

My eyes flit behind him where a crowd is gathering.

One of the tourists from the resort, who I'd noticed looking at Mark curiously several times, says, "Hey, that's Mark Abbott."

I look back at Mark, who hasn't noticed. He's still focused on me.

"Mark," I say firmly, stepping back, but he grabs my hand and drops to one knee in front of me, as if trying to root us in place.

"Please, Frannie. I know it sounds ridiculous, but I was afraid of what we have. What we could be."

The crowd grows, as do the murmurs. And then there's the snapping of cameras. People move closer, trying to get a better shot.

"Mark," I say again, gesturing behind me, but he still doesn't notice.

If we weren't being photographed, it would be sexy as hell how focused he is on me. The sincerity in his eyes tells me how much this means to him, but we can't do this here.

"I promise I'll tell you everything—"

"I'm not saying no to you doing that," I say forcefully. "But I don't think we should do it here." I flare my eyes behind us, and he turns his head to look.

"Shit," he mutters. He looks down at his body and groans when he realizes he's on one knee.

"Should I say yes?" I ask playfully.

"It's either that or slap me. At least it'll give the tabloids a new story to tell. Damn it."

"You really think these people will send pictures to the tabloids?"

"Babe, you have no idea what most people will do for a buck. And right now, I'm worth more than that. Even if they didn't, it would end up on social media and then get picked up, anyway."

"Stand up," I say softly, pulling on his arm.

Slowly, he stands, glancing back at the crowd.

I grab him and spin him to me, then wrap my arms around his neck, his eyes widening as I do.

"How did you find me?"

He gives me a sheepish grin. "I remembered what you told me the first morning here. That you only run when you're angry. And you were pretty pissed at me when you stormed out. Since running on sand sucks, I figured this was where you'd be. To be fair, I did check the beach before I remembered what you said."

"I'm glad you found me." Realizing there's still a growing mob of people staring at us, I say, "Are there some side streets we can take to get back to the resort?"

"You want to go back there with me?"

"Sure. You've got some explaining to do."

His eyes light up, and he smiles, then he kisses my cheek, spins me around and takes one of my hands in his.

"Just don't make me run," I whisper. "I think my feet are bleeding."

"You're ridiculous, babe. Come here." He leads me down a nearby alleyway, then turns at the end of it, putting us on an empty side street. He squats down in front of me. "Climb on."

"What?"

"I'm not letting you walk back with your feet bleeding. Hop on."

When I don't move, he twists his head around to look at me.

"Frannie?"

"Sorry, I..." *I was wrong.*

He shouldn't have lied to me, but I could've let him explain. Holding my hand on the plane wasn't a game. Just like him taking care of me when I had too much to drink or planning a perfect trip to see the dolphins wasn't a game. And neither is this. Those are the most honest parts of him. He's a good man.

With a smile, I climb onto his back and loop my arms around his shoulders. He wraps his arms under my legs and stands up, carrying me back to the resort.

Some of his words may have been lies, but his actions have shown me the truth of who he is.

The kind of man I can picture a future with.

CHAPTER FOURTEEN

Mark

WHEN WE GET BACK to Frannie's room, I set her down next to the bed, then turn to face her, unsure what to expect.

What I see is a soft smile and eyes with a hint of mischief.

She steps closer, running her hand down my chest.

I move in another half step and sweep my hand into her hair, looking into her shining blue eyes.

"I'm sorry."

"I know. You got on one knee for me." She chuckles. "But I want the whole truth. Deal?"

"Deal," I breathe before placing a soft kiss on her lips.

She inhales sharply as she pulls away, starry-eyed.

"*Before* you fuck me, Mark."

My eyes flare. "Oh, really? You still want me to touch you? Hold you?" I drag my lips down her jawline. "Make you come?"

She takes a deep breath and puts her hands on my chest, giving me a little push.

"Only if you tell the whole truth." She shoves me backward. "Nothing but the truth." She pushes me onto the bed and climbs over the top of me, leaning down to whisper in my ear. "So help you God."

Then she jumps off me, kicks off her shoes, and slides under the blankets. "I'm waiting." Her brows dip in as she grimaces, then pulls the blankets back off. Her eyes widen. "And bleeding. Crap. I thought I was joking."

I sit up and see the sheets tinged with blood.

Carefully, I lift one of her feet and see that the heel is completely raw.

"This is why I don't run," she pouts. *Fuck, she's adorable.*

I'm going to make sure she knows exactly how I feel about her. I don't want to lose her. The moment I realized that losing her was far more terrifying than getting into a relationship with her was the moment I knew I had to put it all on the line. Didn't nail it, but I think I've still got a shot.

First, though, her poor heels.

I get off the bed and find the first aid kit in the bathroom. When I get back to her, she's examining the damage.

"Let me see." She's rubbed several layers of skin off her heels and is bleeding lightly. After cleaning them both with hydrogen peroxide, I put on some ointment, and then waterproof bandages.

"Thank you," she says quietly, then she lies down.

Setting everything else on the floor, I lie down next to her, slowly grazing my hand up her thigh as I look into her eyes.

With a reassuring smile, she twines our fingers together and brushes her thumb over my knuckles.

Swallowing the lump that's formed in my throat, I fight past the urge to hide from this. If I want more with her, she deserves the truth. And I want more. God damn, I want all of her.

"I've gotten used to keeping things to myself, to not being vulnerable with anyone who doesn't know me well. In my career, vulnerability is a weakness. People use it to exploit you. I love the sport, but I was never interested in fame. It's a double-edged sword, and I've seen that more than ever these past few weeks."

She listens intently as I explain what happened with Jeff and everything since.

"There's never been a question in my mind about the decision to tell my coach. It was the right thing to do. Punching Jeff, though? I'm starting to worry all the sports analysts out there are right... it cost us the Super Bowl. Something we might never get a shot at again. It drove division on the sidelines that carried over to the field."

She looks at me tenderly.

"I understand why you punched him. You were standing up for someone who didn't have a voice to defend themselves. Believe me, I get it. I've wanted to punch a lot of parents and guardians in my job. People who are supposed to take care of children, but only hurt them. When I see a kid trying not to break down because they're scared of what will happen when they do..." She shakes her head. "I get the urge. And I'm not a football player hyped up with adrenaline and testosterone."

I chuckle at that. "Maybe. I don't know, as much as I enjoyed the shocked look on his face... it doesn't feel good that the game fell apart after that."

"Maybe it was always going to. There's always a catalyst. If it wasn't you, it would've been something else."

"Anyway, I didn't tell you all this because... well, I'm not a crazy person who wants to inundate the person next to me on the plane with every detail of his life. As things went on though, I should've told you, and I'm sorry for that. I was really enjoying not thinking about any of it. I wasn't a football player on the run, I was just Mark. I loved connecting with you without any of that stuff hanging over us. Of course, the flip side is that as we got closer, I was having an internal war about whether it was crazy to have such strong feelings for you so soon."

"And what did you decide?"

"That I can't ignore what we have. Last night, I was going to tell you the truth—tell you everything. But that moment under the stars was so intimate, the words I needed you to hear the most spilled out of me. I want to continue this. Hell, if I'd spent this many days in a row with a girl back home, no doubt she'd be my girlfriend."

It's weird to think like that because it's been so long since someone caught my attention like Frannie has. I've never been the type for games, though. As Grandpa pointed out yesterday, that's not how to treat a woman. Be upfront and honest. I wasn't with Frannie.

"What's stopping you?" she asks.

"What?"

"From asking me to be your girlfriend?"

"You still want that? After all this? Knowing the chaos my life will be?"

"I still want this. I trust you, Mark. No, you shouldn't have continued to lie to me, but you've shown me with your actions who you are, and I'd rather see the truth in them than anywhere else."

Resting my hand on the side of her neck, I guide her toward me, then press my lips into hers.

"I know it's only been a week, but I want more. More of you, more of this, more of us. I want to know what we can be together. Frannie, will you be my girlfriend?"

"I suppose." She playfully rolls her eyes, and damn if that's not a turn on.

I brush my fingers over her ribs, tickling her as she laughs.

"Yes. I would love to be your girlfriend."

In an instant, my mouth is on her plush pink lips. She welcomes the kiss, parting her lips and grazing her tongue over my bottom lip until I deepen the kiss, my tongue swirling over hers.

Call it chemistry or connection, but I've never had it like this with anyone else.

Her hand slides into my hair, and she pulls me closer, molding her body to mine.

Sliding my hand under her shirt, I palm her breast, rubbing my thumb over her nipple, pebbled and poking through the fabric of her bra.

She glides her hand under my shirt, trailing her fingers over my abs before trying to remove my shirt. Which gets stuck because we don't stop our kiss.

"Mm. Take it off," she mutters against my lips.

"You first."

Our lips part just enough for us to frantically remove our shirts, then crash together again.

I unclasp her bra, then pull her shorts down.

She's reaching for mine when my phone goes off.

"Ignore it," I tell her. I'm as hard as stone and have no desire to stop until I'm buried deep inside her, and we've both come so hard we can't move.

She doesn't even acknowledge the noise of my phone, and continues tugging my shorts down.

My phone goes off several more times, and I'm about to throw the damn thing across the room.

Until hers goes off as well. She hesitates for a moment, looking over her shoulder, but then ignores it and turns back to me.

Our eyes meet and I hook my fingers around the edge of her underwear.

Then my phone rings.

"What the fuck?" I yell in its general direction.

Then Frannie's rings.

We stare at each other, then each check our phones, which have both stopped ringing.

"My sister," Frannie says. "A few missed texts from her and Kennedy as well. Oh, and now my mom."

When I look at mine, I see missed texts from Rae, Ackley, Hardy, and my manager—who is also my missed call.

Flipping to the text from my manager, I see what I'd completely forgotten about.

A picture of me on one knee in front of Frannie with the headline, *Mark Abbott Engaged?*

Fuck my life.

"Like she has any fucking room to talk," Frannie mutters, slamming her phone onto the bed.

Forgetting my own crisis for the moment, I turn to her.

"What's wrong?"

"Oh, just my mother."

I wince. "She saw—"

"Yep. And she wasted no time accusing me of keeping things from her."

"Fuck, I'm sorry, Frannie. I'm sure seeing her daughter all over the internet—"

"That's not why I'm mad. I'm not mad that she saw it. I'm mad that she said that to me. She's the one who kept the truth from me my whole life!"

She throws a hand up in exasperation as I stare at her. Jesus, no wonder she reacted how she did to finding out I lied.

"What do you mean?"

She looks at me, a pained expression on her face and vulnerability shimmering in her eyes.

"My dad isn't my biological father. I only found out a few years ago. My mom kept it from me simply because my bio dad was an ex she didn't like. She walked out. Ghosted him. He searched for me for most of my life." Her voice breaks. "I missed out on all of it. We have a relationship now, but I didn't get to grow up with him, all because she lied. And she doesn't even care that it hurt me. Now for her to accuse me..." she trails off, shaking her head.

I tuck some hair behind her ear as I look into her eyes. "I'm so sorry I lied to you. It's obviously a massive trigger for you."

"It is, but... I need to learn to separate a small inconsequential lie that was done out of protection versus a massive lie that destroys everything. I get worked up about lying and pride myself about not doing it, but when I think about it now, I realize I lie on a daily basis to reassure kids. I never know exactly what's going to happen or when things are going to be okay—if they will—but I say it anyway."

"Because you're trying to help them."

"Exactly. I'm not my mother, and neither are you. I appreciate you apologizing, but I think it's time we both stopped. The thing that hurts the most about it all isn't even the lie. It's the fact that my mother wasn't sorry about it. She didn't even care how much it hurt me—or she didn't show me if she did. That changed my entire perception of her. That's what I hate. Finding out that secret changed my opinion of my mother and shattered my relationship with her."

"You know, she might need to hear you say that. And if you ever want to tell her, I promise to hold your hand while you do it."

"Thank you," she says softly. After a quiet moment, she groans. "Sure we can't just stay here forever? I like living in this bubble."

I kiss her forehead as she nestles against my shoulder. "It's a nice bubble, but we have good lives to get back to. Are you sure you still want to do this with me? Even knowing this is what it might be like?"

She sweeps her hand over my cheek. "Positive. What other people say doesn't bother me. It's our trust in each other that matters."

"And you trust me?"

A slow smile spreads across her face. "Yes, I trust you. Because I know you have a good heart. That's what I trust."

I graze my lips over hers in a gentle kiss. When I pull away, I sigh.

"I suppose we ought to deal with all this."

"Probably," she agrees. Then she kisses me again. "Or maybe... we should stay inside our bubble a little longer."

I pull her against me as we slide down in bed. "I like the sound of that."

"Me too," she mutters against my lips.

Forgetting the lies, the headlines, our phones, and everything else, we collide together, happily enjoying our bubble for a little while longer.

Frannie

I LOVE BEING ON VACATION. I've been ignoring my phone for the better part of the last eighteen hours.

Should I have been? Probably not.

Do I care? Not really.

After reassuring everyone I wasn't engaged, and that I hadn't been harboring a secret relationship with an NFL player, I put my phone on silent and enjoyed my time with Mark.

After the initial burst of texts and calls yesterday, Mark sent a group message to his family, letting them know he wasn't engaged. Given that they're more used to dealing with the press blowing things out of proportion, they quickly switched from freaking out to roasting him. That's when he silenced his phone.

Despite how much I've enjoyed the peace, it's time to face the music, so to speak. I have a video chat planned with Hallie and Kennedy later, and Mark says the guys want to talk to me at some point, but before any of that happens, I owe my parents a phone call.

I texted a bit with my biological father last night. He was relaxed and comforting about the situation and after my brief explanation, he simply said he hoped to meet Mark soon.

I know part of the reason is that we don't have as deep of a relationship. We're still getting to know each other and creating a deeper bond, so he's not going to have big opinions about these things. Or if he does, he doesn't want to scare me away with them. I appreciate that small area of relief, whatever the reason.

"Are you sure you want me here for this?" Mark asks, sitting on the bed beside me.

"They'll want to talk to you. And yesterday you told me you'd hold my hand if I ever wanted to tell my mother the truth of how I felt. It might boil over today. We'll see."

He kisses the side of my head and takes my hand. "I'll hold your hand regardless."

I laugh at that. "I should know that by now. You were willing to hold my hand on the plane when I was a complete stranger having a meltdown. Or do you just have a thing for hands? A hand fetish?"

He kisses me, more than likely to shut me up. "Make the call, or I'll pin you to the bed and show you how easily I can make you come and get myself off without using my hands or yours."

I arch a brow. "You're telling me I have to call my mom when you're threatening me with *such* a good time?"

He brushes his lips over mine, then playfully bites my bottom lip. "Okay then. Consider it a reward for being a good girl."

Shit.

I yank my phone off the bed and find my mother's number as Mark laughs.

He may have won that round, but I'll get him back later. First, though, it's this.

I click on my mom's name and select the video chat option. A moment later, she appears on the screen.

"Well, if it isn't my prodigal daughter," she says with a smile. "Any new engagements I should know about?"

I muster a weak smile. I love my mom, and she's being funny, not mean at all, but some days it's still hard to pretend everything's normal.

"No engagements. I'm sorry you had to see all that on the internet."

"Don't worry about that," my dad says, sticking his head into the frame. He's been the most steadfast throughout me finding out he wasn't my biological dad, calmly reassuring me he'd always be my dad. I'm grateful for that.

"Still, I'm sure you have questions."

"Well, of course. Mostly, how long has this been going on? Was this really a solo vacation?"

"It was a solo vacation. I met Mark on the plane and we hit it off."

Dad laughs and shakes his head. "And you had no clue who he was."

I glare at him. "I'm not a football girl! Or baseball, soccer, basketball—I don't know anything about any of it. The only athletic thing I ever did was gymnastics, and the only sport I know about is tennis."

"Oh my god. I forgot about your obsession with Rafa Nadal," Mom says with a laugh.

Beside me, Mark snickers.

"Oh, do I hear laughter?" Mom asks.

I glance at Mark. "Yes. Mark is sitting next to me. If you promise to behave, you can talk to him."

"We promise," Dad says.

"Mostly," Mom adds.

I roll my eyes, then pull the camera back while leaning closer to Mark.

"Mom, Dad, this is Mark. Mark, these are my parents, Cheyenne and Eddie."

"It's nice to meet you both," he says, looking like a polite small-town boy and not the cocky quarterback I know he can be.

"It's nice to meet you too. I'll start up front by saying that if you're dating my daughter, I expect season tickets." My dad keeps a completely straight face and I do my best not to lose my shit as Mark stares at him in surprise.

"Uh, yeah. We could—"

Dad bursts out laughing. "I didn't think it would be that easy. I don't need season tickets, but I'll take them if you're handing them out."

Mark laughs. "You had me there, but if you'd like to come to a game, I can get you tickets for the box."

"I appreciate that, but I think we can talk more about that later."

"So you two met on the plane?" my mom asks, jumping in.

"Yes, Mom," I say. "He was sitting next to me. I was freaking out about flying, and he was kind enough to calm me down, then we started chatting and hit it off."

"But he didn't tell you who he was?"

"It's not something I open up about right away, especially if someone doesn't recognize me," Mark says. "It's nice to get to know someone without that added layer of complexity."

"But then you carried on a relationship with her built on a lie."

"Mom!"

Mark nods. "It wasn't my intention to lie to her, and when I introduced myself, I had no idea we'd ever see each other again, let alone that we were going to the same resort. I assure you, you don't need to worry about the relationship starting with a lie. Frannie knows everything now."

"I don't think you get to comment on lies at all," I say angrily.

Mark rests his hand on my thigh, both calming me and giving me the strength to say this.

"Frannie—"

"Please listen. Mark and I discussed the initial lie about his life, but even as we got to know each other, he told me about his family and friends and was open about his feelings for me. If anything, I got angrier than I should've when I found out who he was because I don't like lying either because of the way you lied to me. I know you think you were protecting me, but you weren't. You were protecting yourself. And while in some ways I understand that, you never take responsibility for how that hurt me. At least Mark apologized and genuinely wanted to fix things." I sigh, looking down. "I'm sorry I haven't said all this sooner. It's not easy for me."

My mom is surprised, but I'm not sure if it's at what I said, how I said it, or the fact that I said it all in front of Mark.

Dad glances at Mom and rubs her back.

"I never wanted to hurt you, Frannie. For a long time, I hoped he was a deadbeat who never would've wanted you so it meant I'd been protecting you. I know that's terrible, but the guilt has been horrible for me to live with. It's made it harder to apologize. I am sorry for keeping something so important from you for so long."

"I appreciate that. Sometimes it still really upsets me."

"You can tell me that. I know I broke your trust, but I'd rather keep talking about it than you freeze me out—which I know you've been doing sometimes. And *maybe* me lying is why I want to make sure no one else lies to you. I don't want anyone else to hurt you like that."

I stare at her for a moment, genuinely surprised. Her words melt some of the anger I've held on to, reminding me she's still my mom, and she truly was trying to protect me—at least initially.

"I think I was building all this up in my head to a massive conflict."

Mom laughs. "You? Never. I'm sorry, honey." Then she looks at Mark. "And I hope you understand why a lie at the start of your relationship concerns me."

"I do. I'm sure you've seen my name in the press lately, and I can tell you the reasons why are not true. I didn't start a fight with our starting QB over playtime. Frannie knows the details of why, but otherwise I don't feel comfortable discussing the real reason. Even my family doesn't know, but the truth will come out next week. I lied because my name was everywhere and I needed an escape. I didn't expect to meet an incredible woman on the plane that I'd get to escape with. My lie to her was benign, but either way, had I known what she'd end up meaning to me, I'd have told her the truth before the flight was over."

I can't help but smile at that.

"I can understand that," Mom says. "Moving on from all this... Frannie, are you still coming home the same day?"

"We changed our flights around so we can fly back together. Ironically, Mark's extended family lives in Ida, so we're going to spend a couple of days in the city, then he's going to go back up to Ida with me."

"Well, we'd love to meet in person before you go back," Dad says.

"Absolutely," Mark agrees.

"Wonderful. Okay, we'll let you get back to your vacation." Mom looks at me sincerely. "I love you, honey."

"Love you too. See you in a few days."

We all say goodbye, and I end the call, leaning back against the pillows, partly in shock, and mostly relieved.

"How do you feel?" Mark asks.

"Good," I say softly. "Surprised. A little more at peace. I feel a little dumb, too."

"Why?"

"Because I should've talked to her sooner. Just like I should've talked to you instead of jumping to conclusions."

Mark waves a hand. "Both reactions were warranted. But let's work on talking in the future."

"Deal."

He leans down and kisses me, and I grab the back of his neck, pulling him closer.

"Let's work on kissing more too," I whisper against his lips. "And maybe some other things."

"Definitely some other things." He flips me over and pins me to the bed, reminding me yet again why this vacation was one of my best decisions ever.

CHAPTER SIXTEEN
TUESDAY

Mark

"YOU KNOW YOU COULD SILENCE THAT," Frannie says as she walks out of the bathroom.

"Huh?" I ask, turning from the book I'm reading to look at her.

She points to my phone, which has been going off all morning. "Silence it, put on airplane mode, turn it off. Throw it out the window."

I chuckle and close my book. "Sorry. I've honestly learned to tune it out."

The news about Jeff Rucker broke today, and my phone has been blowing up, but I barely notice it. I'm used to my phone blowing up every week after a game. The only time I wanted to turn it off was after we lost the Super Bowl.

Though my name is in the press in a positive way today, it's still out there, and I don't need to see any of it. I already prepped a statement for my agent to send out, so I'm sitting back and ignoring it all for the most part, and enjoying my vacation. It's my solace. The resort is a safe space, and Frannie makes it that much easier to ignore the world.

My phone vibrates again, and Frannie glares at it, then picks it up before crawling over me. "Airplane mode or off? You know your family can reach you here at the resort in an emergency."

I sigh. I'm about to tell her to put it on airplane mode when a video call request pops up. Rolling my eyes, I reach for my phone to silence it, but I stop when I see it's a call from my cousin Rae, who is apparently also a friend of Frannie's. She yelled at me via text when she found out I lied to Frannie, but without getting too far into it, I told her there was a reason.

What I didn't tell her was that she'd understand the reason.

Frannie raises her eyebrows in surprise as I swipe up to answer the call.

"Hey," I say, like my name isn't all over the news today.

Rae's eyes lock on mine. "I'm sorry I yelled at you. I'm not a fan of lying, but I appreciate why you did."

"I figured you would, and thank you."

She stares for a moment, then clears her throat. "You've grown up a lot. I'm proud of you."

"Says my little cousin."

She rolls her eyes hard. "I'm not that much younger than you. Shut up." I laugh, but she shakes her head. "Is Frannie right there?"

She pokes her head into the frame. "Hey, Rae. Is this weird?"

Rae laughs. "Maybe a little, but I can see where you two could be a good fit. Just think, if you'd been able to come to my wedding, you could've met him four months ago. Instead, you had to meet him on a plane, then spend a week hooking up with him without knowing who he really was." Rae smiles sweetly, but her eyes are laced with mischief. As usual. Shit-giving is a time-honored Abbott tradition.

Next to me, Frannie snickers. I'm glad *she's* enjoying this.

Thankfully, she throws me a bone and ruffles my hair. "It's all good. It's not like I know anything about sports ball, anyway. Even if I met him at your wedding, I wouldn't have known who he was, and if he tried to act like a big deal, I would've rolled my eyes."

Rae attempts and fails at stifling a laugh. "Yep. Perfect match. This is awesome."

Pain in my ass.

"What's awesome?" a voice from behind Rae calls. Then her sister Sarah appears in the frame. "Oh, hi Frannie!"

"Good to see you too," I mutter. Frannie laughs. Sarah and Rae laugh. *I guess I'll just go fuck myself.*

"Is that Mark?" another voice calls, and then Dani squishes into the frame as well.

"Wow, it's like a clown car," Frannie says with a laugh.

"You promise everything's okay? Because we can kick his butt if he's not behaving," Rae says.

"You're going to kick a professional quarterback's ass?" Frannie asks, mirth in her eyes.

"There are a lot of Abbotts," Dani says with a wicked smile.

I turn the phone back toward me. "Could you take it down about ten notches?"

"Nope," Sarah says, popping the P. "You always grill the people we date to make sure they're treating us right. We're just making sure you're treating Frannie right."

"But *I'm* your cousin," I protest. "Shouldn't you be worrying about her being good to me?"

They all laugh and shake their heads. "No. If she's happily sticking around after all the crazy you put her through, she must really like you," Rae says sweetly.

"What if I'm a stalker?" Frannie asks. At least someone is on my team.

Dani waves a hand. "Then he can take you. He's a pro-football quarterback after all." Dani winks, and I'm about to throw my phone across the room. There's nothing quite like a roasting from my family.

"Wow, this has been a great chat, but my battery is dying, so we should go."

"Liar," Sarah says with a smile.

"It's flashing the warning light," I say dramatically.

"Can't take a little harmless teasing?" Dani asks.

"Oh, I think it's about to power down."

"Dinner when you get back to Ida," Rae says, locking eyes with me.

Sighing, I say, "Yeah. Of course." Then I smile. "Oh no, I'm losing you. Bye!"

Then I hang up as Frannie laughs.

I shake my head and toss my phone to the side. "They're crazy."

"They're hilarious," she counters.

"Enjoy it now. It won't be so funny when you're surrounded by a million of them all asking you questions about how we met and when we're getting married."

She lifts an eyebrow. "They know we're not actually engaged, right?"

"Yep. It won't change the questions."

She laughs and shakes her head. "I'll start humming Eminem songs and let my crazy meet theirs."

Leaning over, I give her a kiss. "You *are* crazy. My kind of crazy." My phone goes off again, but I silence it with one hand, dragging my other thumb across her cheek. "Thanks for putting up with all the insanity in my life. God, one week and you've already been in the news."

"Ten days, and what's life without a little paparazzi stalking? I can handle it. As long as they don't touch me, come on my property, and always catch a good shot of my butt, I'll be fine."

"I'm so glad I sat down next to you on that plane and didn't switch seats the second I saw you rocking back and forth."

"Best decision of your life," she says with a smirk. Then she gives me one more quick kiss before climbing off the bed and extending her hand to me. "Now, what do you say we go down to the beach and enjoy what's left of our vacation?"

Our vacation.

I came here single, tired, and ready to be out of the eye of the press.

In two days I'm going to leave here, still with all eyes on me but no longer single or tired. I'm rejuvenated, filled with joy, and falling hard for a girl I never expected to sweep into my life, tackle my heart, and knock the wind out of me.

Taking her hand, I stand up, leaving my phone behind as we head for the door.

"Sounds perfect to me."

CHAPTER SEVENTEEN
THURSDAY

Frannie

"WHAT TIME DOES your flight get in?" Hallie asks over the video call I'm on with her and Kennedy.

"Around two, but we're heading back to Mark's place to drop off our stuff before we come to your apartment."

"Why are we having dinner at our place, then? Shouldn't we be at Mark's swanky penthouse?" Kennedy asks.

I roll my eyes. "It's not a penthouse." It is massive and gorgeous, though. At least from the pictures he showed me. "It's just a condo."

The phone lifts from my hand and Mark holds it up to his face. "Don't let her downplay it. It's stunning," he teases.

I bump his elbow with mine. "Don't hype them up."

"Aw, come on, babe. It's fun. You know, we could all get together at my place. Brian and Hardy want to meet you."

Kennedy's hand shoots up. "I vote for yes!"

Mark looks at me as Hallie wiggles excitedly.

"Fine," I agree. "But I don't want to hear about it when you have to keep Hardy on a leash," I tell him.

Over the last few days of our vacation, we had multiple video chats with Hardy and Brian, and with Hallie and Kennedy. The boys just wanted to get a glimpse of me, and the girls needed to give their stamp of approval for Mark.

As soon as his gorgeous face was on the call with them, they lost their desire to give him shit, though they did their cursory warning that if he breaks my heart, they'll sell all his secrets to the press. Probably more of a threat than them breaking his face.

Kennedy and Hallie are still cheering about getting to spend the evening with hot football players. It might be a recipe for disaster, but hopefully it'll be fun.

Tomorrow morning, we're having brunch with my parents, then heading back to Ida. Mark said he could stay with his grandparents, but I told him I liked our bubble, and maybe we could keep it up in my apartment. It might be crazy, but I've spent twelve straight days with him on vacation and I've enjoyed it all. I don't want to stop. Plus, I'll be at work all day during the week. I want him in my apartment—and definitely my bed—every night.

Though I was supposed to stay in Anais Bay for ten days, and Mark for a full two weeks, we both changed our plans, opting to stay for twelve days and fly back together. Mark sprung for first class seats saying if he has to put up with the downsides of his job —like endless banter about him in the press—then he might as well enjoy the perks, too.

There's an announcement through the PA system that our flight is boarding, so I take the phone back from Mark. "We've got to go. We'll see you in a few hours. I'll text you Mark's address and the time!"

"Okay, love you," Kennedy says.

"Try not to cry on the plane this time," Hallie adds.

"Hey! I did not cry last time."

"No," Mark says, poking his head into the frame. "She was a champ. And she will be again."

He kisses my cheek and I blush.

The girls ooh and aww.

"Okay, on that note, goodbye!"

They wave and I hang up, shaking my head. Mark hands me a coffee, then stands and grabs my carry-on before taking my hand.

I stand up, and together we walk toward the boarding area.

"What are we going to cook?" I ask. "Can you cook?"

"Tonight? Well, we could just order in. But yeah, I can cook. Pasta."

I raise my eyebrows at him. "That's such a guy thing to say."

He takes mock offense to my statement. "Excuse me. I don't mean I can boil noodles."

"Oh, I'm so sorry. Please forgive me."

The attendant snickers at our conversation as we hold out our phones for him to scan our boarding passes. Mark leads the way up the ramp to the plane.

"I'm serious," he says. "Look, I learned from my dad at a young age how to cook meat. Steak, chicken, pork chops. No problem. Except for when I got tired of eating bread or potatoes on the side. My mother told me learning to make different kinds of pasta sauces was the key. Once I learned that, I could have a different pairing for every type of meat I make. So, I know how to make pasta. I make a killer chicken marsala."

I love chicken marsala.

"Okay, I'm impressed. I expect that to be the first meal you make me because it's one of my favorites."

"Deal."

My mouth drops as we enter the first class section. Large plush tan seats with extendable footrests and large TV screens sit in front of us. *I could get used to flying.* Well, I could get used to first class, at least. Not sure I'll ever get used to flying, but as long as Mark is sitting next to me, I might be okay with it.

I must not have been paying very close attention when I boarded my last flight, probably because I was too nervous. Otherwise, I would've remembered this.

"Nice, huh?"

"Mhm," I nod.

"You want the window?" he asks.

To my surprise, I say, "Yes. It might sound weird, but the light coming in makes me feel less claustrophobic."

"You just don't want to stare out the window."

"Correct," I say, sitting down and tucking my purse under the seat.

"You're so weird." He sits down next to me and extends his legs.

"You like it," I tease.

He sits up and gives me that same sexy smolder that captivated me on the plane ride down here. Then his hand is on my thigh and I'm feeling a bit dazed.

"Yeah, I do," he rumbles before kissing me. When he pulls away, he takes my hand. "So, tell me, can *you* cook?"

"Pasta," I say, fighting back a laugh.

"Just pasta?"

"Honestly, I'm a great salad maker and baker, but ask me to cook anything on a stovetop and I'll burn it. There's a reason I eat at Marion's so much."

"Sounds like we're the perfect match."

"I guess we are."

He leans in and kisses me again, then he looks past me out the window.

"Ready for your second flight?" he asks.

I glance at the window and take a deep breath. "As I can be."

"Uh oh. Do I need to distract you?"

I shrug. "Wouldn't hurt."

He leans in to kiss me, when there's a voice from the aisle.

"Oh my. Maybe those engagement rumors were right."

We look up to see a smiling woman who looks to be in her sixties.

"Leave them alone, sweetheart. The last thing they need is someone gawking," a man behind her says.

But she smiles at us. "Whatever the reason, you look very happy, and that's always something to enjoy. Take care."

Mark and I both smile.

"Thanks, you too," I tell her.

"Sorry about that," the man behind her, presumably her husband, says. Then he looks at Mark earnestly. "I don't want to bother you, but I want to say I respect what you did, taking the blame for things, protecting that woman. It speaks to your character." He pats Mark on the shoulder. "Have a good flight."

"You too," Mark says in surprise, though I don't know why. Since the news broke two days ago, Mark has become a fan favorite again. Though we avoided reading much about it, we did read the press release from his coach absolving Mark of any blame and explaining why Mark did what he did. Jeff Rucker was arrested on the same day, and his wife had divorce papers served. Justice, if you ask me. As usual, though, Mark just wants to fly under the radar.

Squeezing his hand again, I draw his attention back to me.

"Okay?" I ask.

He nods. "Funny enough, they reminded me of my grandparents. My grandpa would've gone out of his way to say something like that as well. Although it probably would've been more profound. Like his whole fate speech."

"Fate speech?" I ask.

"The gist? When fate sneaks up on you and smacks you across the face, it always leaves a mark."

At that, I laugh. "Well, it definitely left a Mark on me."

He shakes his head. "Your jokes are so bad."

"Again I say, you like it."

"Maybe," he says, eyes dancing. He leans in and kisses me again, then he looks past me out the window. "Feeling any better now?"

I glance at the window and take a deep breath. "A little."

"Well, you've already got my hand. I'm happy to distract you however you'd like." He gives me a cheeky smile. "And once we're in the air, you can always order a drink."

"Uh, no. Alcohol and I are still on a break," I tell him, trying to forget the night of puking. "But either way, I don't need it this time."

"Not scared anymore?"

Glancing down at our intertwined hands, I smile.

"It's still scary, but now I know it's worth it."

He looks at me adoringly, then squeezes my hand and kisses my cheek.

"Damn right it is. Worth every second."

Mark

I'VE JUST STEPPED out of the bathroom in Frannie's apartment when the front door opens and the heavenly scent of Marion's chicken soup hits my nostrils.

"That smells delicious," I say, walking over to Frannie and taking the bags from her hands. I lean down for a kiss, which she happily gives me.

"Me or the food?" she asks with a grin.

"Both. But right now, I'm starving."

"Have a good run?" she asks, knowing I've been running in the afternoons when the weather is warmest around here. I've also learned to take my time because the odds of running into someone I know—especially a family member—are high around here.

When we get to the kitchen, Frannie sets a paper down on the kitchen table.

I groan when I see what it is. "Why do you have one of these crappy tabloids?"

"Because I'm on it."

I roll my eyes. "Your ass is on it," I say, looking at the photos of us hugging and kissing. While my face is visible in a few photos, only her back—and yes, her gorgeous ass—are showing. "No one is going to know it's you."

She turns around in mock offense. "Excuse me. Do you know how many times I've asked Hallie and Kennedy to check what my ass looks like in the mirror? They'll know."

I stare at her for a moment. I'm head over heels for this girl.

"What?" she asks, setting some spoons down on the table.

I walk over and wrap my arms around her, giving her a deep kiss. "I love you," I whisper against her lips.

Her eyebrows shoot up, eyes flared as she looks at me. "What?"

Sweeping some hair off her shoulder, I cup her cheek and look into her eyes, making sure she knows these words are the absolute truth. "I love you, Frannie."

Her eyebrows drop, and her lips curve up, growing into a radiant smile. She throws her arms around my neck. "I love you too, Mark."

She jumps up, wrapping her legs around my waist and kissing me deeply.

I carry her over to the kitchen counter and set her on it as my tongue delves greedily into her mouth. This girl is all fucking mine. Offering her my hand on the plane was the best thing I ever did. I might not have believed it at the time, but now I know the truth. We were meant to sit next to each other that day. Meant to fall hard on vacation. Meant to come back here and do the work of building a solid relationship. I've only known her for seven weeks, but I know with certainty, this crazy girl is my future.

My family loves her too. Once I explained the engagement rumor nonsense—which my family was less concerned about given how familiar they are with my job—they were just excited to meet her. We had a mini family reunion at my parents' house a couple of weekends ago, and Frannie fit in perfectly. Further proof this girl was made for me. She can handle the wild Abbott clan. And she's more than willing to work with my football schedule and figure out how best to make our relationship work without either of us needing to sacrifice too much in our careers. That'll all come in time, though. For now, I'm enjoying kissing the woman I love, falling asleep with her in my arms every night, and living a life I love.

There's a vibration against my hand, and I pull Frannie's phone from her back pocket and hand it to her. Reluctantly pulling her lips from mine, she takes it and checks it. Then she laughs.

"Ha! Told you!" She holds out the phone, and I read a couple of texts from Hallie and Kennedy.

> **HALLIE**
>
> Saw your ass on Insta this morning! Looking hot, sis!
>
> **KENNEDY**
>
> Oh! I saw it in line at the deli at lunch. I told the cashier it was my cousin's ass. The jerk didn't believe me.

"Told you they'd know my ass anywhere." She sets the phone down and looks up at me proudly as I shake my head.

"Crazy. In the best way." I kiss her forehead. "And I love you."

She sighs dreamily. "I love you too. I'm going to say that all the time now."

"Same. Come on." I take her hand and she hops off the counter, then follows me over to the kitchen table.

Grabbing the paper, she says, "I didn't actually buy it because of my ass." She flips to the second page and slides it in front of me. "Not everything in there is a lie. And I liked seeing that."

I read the headline.

The New York Bandits confirmed today that Mark Abbott will serve as starting quarterback this year following the firing of Jeff Rucker after his arrest for multiple counts of sexual assault.

"They love you again," she says with a laugh.

"I guess they do."

She tilts her head and looks at me. "What?"

"Nothing. Just... hard to believe how things work out sometimes. I never would've imagined this is how I'd end up QB1 or that I'd be here with you, but I'm happier than I've ever been."

"Me too." She pulls the lid off the container of soup and shrugs. "Guess that's fate."

When fate sneaks up and smacks you across the face, it always leaves a mark.

Grandpa was right. But the mark it left didn't change me, it simply helped me realize what I wanted and gave me the push to fight for it.

I look back at Frannie and smile.

Best decision ever.

The End

Need a little Mark & Frannie bonus chapter?
Want more from the Baker Girls?
Want to know more about the Abbott family?
Find it all & more here:

A NOTE FROM BETHANY

Thanks so much for reading! I hope you enjoyed this fun, beachy romance and all of Mark and Frannie's shenanigans. If you want more from Mark and Frannie, grab their bonus epilogue on my website.

If you're looking for more from the Baker Girls, don't miss Kennedy and Devon's BFFs to lovers romance, The Last Key, plus stories for Justin, Hallie, and Hardy & Ackley.
And if you want to know more about the Abbott family, start the Friends Like This series which begins with Rae and Aaron's epic four book love story before moving into Sarah and Joel's friends to lovers romance. You'll find plenty of wise and snarky words from Gram and Grandpa throughout.

For more news, updates on what I'm working on, teasers, and freebies, sign up for my newsletter or hop over to my reader group, Bethany Monaco Smith's Book Besties
Thanks again for reading!
XO,
Bethany

THE LAST LIE PLAYLIST

You can find the playlist for The Last Lie on Spotify

- Vacation- The Go-Go's
- Lose Yourself- Eminem
- Catch- Brett Young
- A Little Lime- Jordan Davis
- Gimme That Sunshine- Animal Island
- Island In The Sun- Weezer
- Jump Then Fall (Taylor's Version)- Taylor Swift
- One Of Them Girls- Lee Brice
- Beachin'- Jake Owen
- She Likes It- Russell Dickerson, Jake Scott
- Slow Down Sunrise- Ryan Griffin
- Can't Help Falling in Love- Haley Reinhart
- TRUSTFALL- P!nk
- So Do I- Jordan Davis
- Dandelions- Ruth B.
- Beautiful Crazy- Luke Combs
- Love is Real- Morgan Evans
- My Person- Brandon Ray

BETHANY'S BOOKS

Freaking Love series
First Love
Real Love
Forever Love

Friends Like This series
Friends Like This
Falling Like This
Broken Like This
Love Like This
Married Like This
(a Friends Like This bonus novella)
Together Like This
Heartbreak Like This
Family Like This
Future Like This
Nothing Like This
Trust Like This
Always Like This

Ida Heartthrobs series
The Forever Fight
The Perfect Love
The Future Play

Baker Girls series
The Last Lie
The Last Key
The Last Love Story
The Last Thing
The Last Person

Ida Romance series
Reckless for You
Faking It for the Holidays
Waiting for Your Heart
(free novella)
Everything for You
Running Back to You
Stealing Your Perfect Heart
(free short story)
Caught Up In Your Love

Lacy Creek series
Finally Yours
Always Mine
Only Ours
Complete Trilogy

Standalone
Fake It Till You Fall
(free novella)
Lost In My Heart
(free short story)

ABBOTT FAMILY TREE

Pete & Bea Abbott

- **Chris & Cynthia Abbott**
  - Mason (Taylor) Abbott
  - Cole (Justine) Abbott
  - Andrea Abbott
  - Mark Abbott

- **Sylvia & Eric Malone**
  - Weston Malone
  - Dani Malone
  - Olivia Malone

- **Darren & Lindsay Abbott**
  - Cassie Abbott
  - Lincoln Abbott
  - Kyle Abbott
  - Tori Abbott

- **Kara & Charlie McKinley**
  - Rae (Aaron) Cooper
  - Sarah McKinley

ABOUT THE AUTHOR

Bethany Monaco Smith is a writer-mom. When she's not busy hanging with her boys, she's writing beautifully messy love stories.

She loves happily-ever-afters and cries at every emotional moment, whether reading, writing, or watching. When she's not mom-ing or writing, you can find her binge-reading on Kindle Unlimited, supporting fellow indie authors, and having sushi dates with her SIL. Bethany survives on coffee, rewatching the same TV shows over and over, and her KU subscription. She lives in the Southern Tier of NY with her husband and two sons.

For more about Bethany and what she's working on, follow along on Instagram or on her website, bethanymonacosmith.com. Stay in touch by joining Bethany's exclusive Facebook group, Bethany's Book Besties & signing up for her newsletter.

ACKNOWLEDGMENTS

Cassie, thank you for keeping me on track, saying yes when I ask if we can do some crazy thing in a short amount of time, and always reminding me to take it easy on myself. You are the best!

Lacey, thank you as always for the thoughtful edits, and more importantly your friendship. Love you!

Shani, for always reading and giving me all the notes! Mark is yours.

The BOD squad for your endless support, cheering me on, and lifting me up. You are THE BEST. All the hearts.

To all my betas, thank you for your feedback and thoughts, and helping to make this story shine!

To my supremely awesome ARC/Street team, THANK YOU. You ladies are the absolute best and I could not do all this without you!

To the incredible author/bookish community I'm lucky to be a part of, thank you. You have been a source of camaraderie, support, and hilarious memes that keep me going on the rough days and celebrate with me on the awesome ones. Y'all are the best!

Finally, to all of you for picking up this book, reading this story, and (if you've read this far) hopefully falling in love with these characters. I appreciate every one of you!